D0227040

LLYFRGELL CEREDIGION LIBRARY
38021962548274

SPECIAL MESSAGE TO READERS

This book is published under the auspices of

THE ULVERSCROFT FOUNDATION

(registered charity No. 264873 UK)

Established in 1972 to provide funds for research, diagnosis and treatment of eye diseases. Examples of contributions made are: —

A Children's Assessment Unit at Moorfield's Hospital, London.

•

Twin operating theatres at the Western Ophthalmic Hospital, London.

•

A Chair of Ophthalmology at the Royal Australian College of Ophthalmologists.

•

The Ulverscroft Children's Eye Unit at the Great Ormond Street Hospital For Sick Children, London.

You can help further the work of the Foundation by making a donation or leaving a legacy. Every contribution, no matter how small, is received with gratitude. Please write for details to:

THE ULVERSCROFT FOUNDATION,
The Green, Bradgate Road, Anstey,
Leicester LE7 7FU, England.
Telephone: (0116) 236 4325

In Australia write to:

THE ULVERSCROFT FOUNDATION,
c/o The Royal Australian and New Zealand
College of Ophthalmologists,
94-98 Chalmers Street, Surry Hills,
N.S.W. 2010, Australia

THE CALL OF HOME

Shortly after arriving in Australia Dr Tam Lawrence falls ill with an ectopic pregnancy. An operation leaves her unable to have children and so she breaks off her relationship with Dr Matt Nelson in the UK without telling him why. When she returns to the UK things are cool between them — but then Tam is called out to a motorcycle accident. Believing the badly injured rider is Matt, she can no longer deny her feelings for him . . .

Books by Teresa Ashby
in the Linford Romance Library:

LOVE ON ICE
FOR THE CHILDREN'S SAKE

TERESA ASHBY

THE CALL OF HOME

Complete and Unabridged

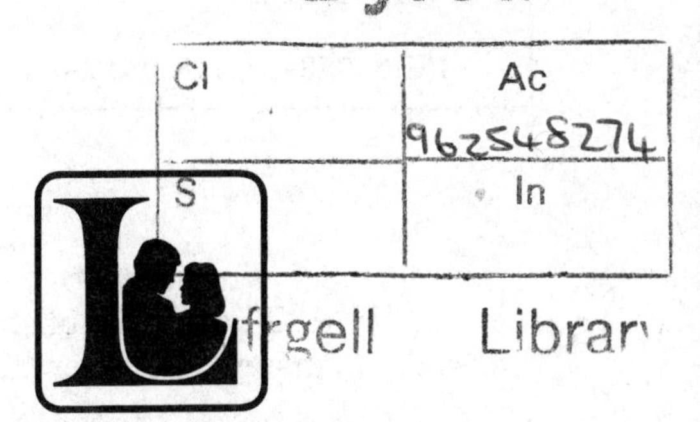

LINFORD
Leicester

First published in Great Britain in 2010

First Linford Edition
published 2011

British Library CIP Data

Ashby, Teresa.
The call of home. - -
(Linford romance library)
1. Physicians- -Fiction.
2. Love stories
3. Large type books.
I. Title II. Series
823.9'2–dc22

ISBN 978–1–4448–0630–4

Published by
F. A. Thorpe (Publishing)
Anstey, Leicestershire

Set by Words & Graphics Ltd.
Anstey, Leicestershire
Printed and bound in Great Britain by
T. J. International Ltd., Padstow, Cornwall

This book is printed on acid-free paper

1

'Are you all right, Tam?' Cara's concerned voice seemed to be coming from a very long way away.

Tam licked her lips. This wasn't meant to be happening. She hadn't been here long, and the last thing she wanted everyone to think was that she couldn't cope with the work.

'I — I'm not sure,' Tam replied.

She'd been feeling off colour for a few days, but today she'd suddenly started to feel much worse. A few moments ago, her head had started to spin and her vision had blurred.

And she didn't even want to think about that persistent pain in her side that had been getting steadily worse.

I can't be *ill*, she thought as Cara's face swam before her. *I have patients to see, things to do.*

'Sit down for a minute,' Cara ordered briskly.

Tam sank onto a chair and gulped back a wave of nausea. She managed to thank Cara in a voice little more than a hoarse croak.

'You haven't felt well for a while, have you?' Cara said. 'You've been looking decidedly peaky. Are you in pain?'

Tam nodded. 'A little,' she whispered, knowing she was understating the severity of it as her hand slid to the left side of her abdomen. 'It's just a stomach upset, that's all.'

'Sickness? Diarrhoea?'

'Some,' Tam admitted. 'It's nothing, Cara, honestly. I had a hectic few weeks before I left the UK, then there was the long flight.'

'It may just be that you need a break, but I'd like to do a blood test just to be sure. In the meantime, lie down in a cubicle for a while,' Cara said.

Should have seen a doctor before, Tam thought, then laughed somewhat desperately. *I am a doctor! Should have recognised the signs*. Something was definitely not right here and it was beginning to frighten her.

She was barely aware of Cara drawing some blood. There were other things going on, too. Poking, prodding . . . was this what it was like to be on the other side?

She'd heard Cara say something about a 'tender mass' and didn't even want to think about what that might mean.

She tried to relax, recalling a technique to go in one's mind to somewhere familiar and peaceful. The rushing noise in her ears became the shuffle of the shingle beneath gentle summer waves, the burning heat in her face turned into the warmth of the sun.

She was in Heron Bay, on the beach beneath the cliffs.

Way up behind her stood Bay House. Home. Bay House had never been her home, but it was the one place she could always run to if she needed a bolthole. She felt safe there. Loved. No wonder she had found her way there, in her mind at least.

Pain oozed through the dream. Tam squeezed her eyes shut, bit her lip and added another element to her vision of peace and tranquillity. He was walking along the beach towards her, dark hair ruffled by the breeze. Oh, how she loved him — how she needed him.

'Matt,' she whispered.

He knelt down behind her and wrapped his arms around her. She could almost feel the warmth of his lips against her skin. *Help me, Matt . . .*

'Are you still with us, Tam?' Cara's pleasant but insistent Australian voice broke through her jumbled thoughts.

Tam knew she had to make an effort, but she didn't want to leave Heron Bay and Matt behind. It was bad enough that everything she loved was thousands of miles away, surely she hadn't to leave her dreams behind too?

But Cara had been good to her, putting her up at her house, taking her under her wing at the hospital.

'I think I may be rather ill,' she whispered as Cara's concerned face swam into vision.

'I'm afraid you may be right,' Cara said.

'I'm so dry. Could I have a drink?'

'Sorry, you're not to have anything. Did you eat breakfast this morning?'

Tam tried to remember. Why was it important whether she ate breakfast or not? Who cared? All she wanted was for the pain to go away. It was consuming her now, like a fire raging throughout her body.

'Tam,' Cara persisted. 'Did you eat anything?'

'I did,' Tam said. 'But I didn't keep it down.'

Cara sighed. 'Did you know you were pregnant, Tam?'

'Pregnant? No, not possible,' Tam said, feeling more confused than ever. 'I can't be.'

'Listen, Tam,' Cara said, her voice grave. 'You are pregnant, but your uterus is empty. You understand what this means? I'm sorry, Tam, but . . . '

Panic set in. Pregnant? Then not pregnant?

Tam realised what Cara was talking about. Ectopic pregnancy. Poor little baby, trapped in the wrong place — no chance of survival. As the truth sank in, despair washed over her in a huge overwhelming rush.

'Oh, Matt,' she sobbed and turned her face to the pillow as hot tears coursed down her face. 'I'm so sorry.'

'Tam. Is there anyone you'd like me to inform? The father perhaps?'

'Father?' Tam wept. Father of what? 'No,' she murmured. 'No one must know about this, Cara. No one.'

She tried to sit up. The pain was bad now; every movement was agony.

'They'll try for a repair,' Cara said. 'The tube will only be removed as a last resort. You're in good hands here, Tam, you know that.'

'I know,' Tam whispered hoarsely.

Right now she wanted Matt here to

hold her hand, tell her that everything was going to be all right. Or did she? Did she really want him to drop everything and rush to Australia for all the wrong reasons? He'd been planning to join her as soon as things could be arranged.

But there wasn't time to think about all that now.

She gripped Cara's cool hand tightly.

'Don't tell anyone from home,' she said urgently. 'They mustn't know about this.'

* * *

As always, Matt sat by the phone, staring at it willing the hands on the clock to move faster so he could call Tam.

He smiled. He was thirty-two, but he felt like a lovesick boy of seventeen. Just the thought of her made his heart beat faster, his stomach tighten with longing. If only she weren't so far away. If only they'd had more than that one night together before she had to leave.

He'd promised to follow her to Australia as soon as he could.

His smile widened. She was expecting this call from him, and he had good news for her. Andrew had agreed to him taking leave, and locum cover had been arranged. All being well, Matt would be joining Tam in Sydney within the next two weeks.

He couldn't wait to tell her the news. He glanced at the clock. Ten minutes to go — but he couldn't wait any longer and grabbed the phone.

He was almost at the point of hanging up when the phone was picked up.

'Cara Stanford.'

'Cara? Hi!' he said warmly. 'Pleased to speak to you at last. I'm Matt Nelson. Is Tam there?'

'Tam?' Cara sucked in her breath and he sensed something was wrong.

'She is all right isn't she?'

'Um, sure, she's fine, Matt,' Cara said. 'She's . . . '

Alarm bells began to ring in Matt's mind. 'What is it?' he said.

'There's been a bit of an emergency at the hospital,' Cara explained. 'Tam's likely to be tied up there for some time. I'll get her to call you as soon as she can. Is there a message?'

A message? Matt felt more than disappointed. He wanted, needed, to hear her voice.

'Just tell her I love her,' he said at last. 'Tell her to call me anytime, day or night because I must talk to her. Tell her I have news for her. Good news.'

He walked over to the window that looked out over the sea and, placing one hand on the frame either side, leaned his head against the cool glass. The water looked as if it had been sprinkled with tiny stars that shimmered in the sunshine and there wasn't a cloud to be seen in the sky.

What kind of emergency would have kept Tam at the hospital so late at night when her consultant was at home? He pushed himself away from the window and turned and stared at the phone. If she'd changed her mind about him, about them, he wasn't sure he could bear it.

* * *

'Call him,' Cara said a few days later. 'I can't keep telling the poor guy you're caught up in an emergency at the hospital. He's starting to suspect something is going on. Just put him out of his misery, please, Tam.'

'It's only been four days,' Tam murmured.

She wished with all her heart that Cara would leave her alone with her misery. She didn't want to talk to anyone, least of all Matt. Tears pricked her eyes when she thought of him. Dear Matt, who had spent his whole life longing for a normal family life.

As a child, he'd yearned for a stable home, and the only constant for him back then had been the summers spent at her Uncle Andrew's house.

It had been the same for Tam. Her mother had been only too pleased to offload her for the summer with her Aunt Moira, Uncle Andrew and her cousin Jack.

Matt was Jack's best friend, and just as much a summer fixture at Heron Bay as Tam. They were a pair of loose ends, a couple of lonely kids who came alive in the summer.

And now Matt was an adult, his yearning had turned towards a wife and children. He wanted to give his children the kind of life he'd missed.

'Four days is a long time when you're worried,' Cara said, holding the phone towards Tam. 'Talk to the man. When he's spoken to me, he sounds as if he's in pieces, Tam. Tell him you love him. You do, don't you?'

'More than anything,' Tam whispered. 'That's why I can't . . . '

'Can't what?' Cara cried in exasperation.

Tam lowered her eyes. 'He wants a family.'

'That's it? That's what's holding you back? Oh, heaven save us, Tam, what am I to do with you? If he knew how ill you'd been, how close we'd come to losing you, do you honestly believe he'd be worried about having kids? And there are alternatives. I shouldn't have to tell you that.'

Tam dragged her gaze up to look at Cara, her soft grey eyes laden with misery. How could she understand? How could anyone who hadn't been through it know how she felt? How could she deny the man she loved the future he'd always longed for?

'Oh, love, you look so sad,' Cara murmured. 'Matt knows something is wrong. You have to talk to him.'

Tam fought back her sorrow. It was time to stop feeling sorry for herself. After all, she was still alive, wasn't she?

In the end they had been unable to perform a laparoscopy and Tam had undergone major abdominal surgery. It may have been 'an ectopic', but it was still a baby, a life created by her and

Matt. She needed time to mourn, time to get her disordered thoughts into some kind of shape.

'Call him,' Cara insisted.

Tam took the phone. 'Okay,' she agreed with a small smile.

Tam sat for a long time cradling the telephone in her hands, thinking over what she had to say. Maybe she was being silly, thinking that she was about to break Matt's heart. It had just been one night, after all. Just one night.

Just because it had felt to her as if she'd held the moon and stars in her hands, didn't necessarily mean that those feelings had gone so deep for Matt. After all, guys were different, weren't they? Her cousin Jack, still Matt's best friend, was a case in point.

Love 'em and leave 'em, that was Jack's motto. Who was to say Matt was any different?

It would be late evening at home. A good time to catch Matt. She tapped out his number.

'Aunt Moira,' she said, feeling her

voice catch in her throat. Just hearing that warm, familiar voice almost broke her heart.

'Hello, darling,' Moira replied. She was a dear lady, and Tam was closer to her than she'd ever been to her own mother. 'We were just talking about you earlier. No one's heard from you for a while. We were wondering how you were. They're not working you too hard, are they? Matt says he's had the devil's own job trying to speak to you.'

'What are you doing at Matt's cottage?'

'We had dinner here,' Moira explained. 'But Matt was called out on an emergency. He's likely to be a while.'

'Aunt Moira,' Tam said, her mouth suddenly as dry as a bone. She licked her parched lips. 'Is Uncle Andrew with you?'

'He's in the kitchen making coffee. Why, what is it, dear? You sound upset. Has something happened?'

Tension crackled along the line.

Moira was too good at sensing things. She seemed to know instinctively that something was wrong.

'Aunt Moira, please don't tell Matt this . . . he must never know, but . . . '

'What, dear? What's happened?'

This wasn't what she'd intended at all, but hearing her aunt's familiar voice had overwhelmed her fragile defences and the whole story came flooding out. Tam hadn't meant to tell her. In fact, she'd planned to go home at the end of her year away and not mention a word of this to anyone.

There was no condemnation from Moira — just heartfelt sympathy.

'But of course, Matt must be told,' she said when Tam had finished speaking. 'The man is deeply in love with you. I've never seen him so happy — or so miserable — as he's been these past months. He's been absolutely lost, and yet he's never without a smile on his face. He'd want to know.'

'No, Aunt Moira,' Tam said firmly. 'Absolutely not. He must never know.

Please, promise me you won't breathe a word?'

'I don't know,' Moira sighed. Tam knew without even seeing her that Moira would be chewing on her lip. 'I love you both so much. I think you're wrong to keep him in the dark about this.'

'But it's my decision,' Tam said as panic began to seep in. She couldn't tell Matt now. He'd want to know why she hadn't told him straight away and she didn't have an answer for him. He'd think she didn't trust him and he'd be hurt and she didn't want to hurt him.

She swallowed back tears. 'Matt must never know,' she repeated firmly.

'If you're sure that's what you really want,' Moira said, her disapproval perfectly clear in the tone of her voice. 'But I think you're wrong, Tam.'

She broke off and spoke to her husband, who must have just entered the room with the coffee.

'Don't tell Uncle Andrew either, please, Aunt Moira,' Tam begged urgently. 'Let this just be between us. He'll only worry.'

'Of course, dear,' Moira replied. 'Don't worry. Keep in touch now, won't you? And take care.'

'I will. Thank you, Aunt Moira,' Tam said. 'And if Matt has any plans to come out here, please talk him out of it.'

'Well, of course he has plans,' Moira said, her voice muffled as if she was trying to prevent her husband overhearing. 'What am I supposed to say to him? You're putting me in a very difficult situation.'

'I know and I'm so sorry . . . '

There was a deep sigh. 'No, I'm the one who should be sorry,' Moira answered. 'You've been through a terrible ordeal, all on your own, no one to turn to. It's easy for me to sit in judgment when I'm so far away. Oh, darling, I wish I could just give you a big hug.'

'I do, too,' Tam said, her voice cracking as the tears she'd been fighting so hard began to spill down her cheeks.

'Leave it with me, dear,' Moira said briskly. 'I'll think of something. You're not to worry about a thing.'

Suddenly Tam felt drained. The nurse was on her way round to take her blood pressure and temperature and it was time to end the call.

The nurse frowned. 'Your temp's up a bit,' she said.

'I'm not surprised,' Tam replied, turning her face into her pillow.

* * *

Returning home, Matt was surprised to see the living room lights still blazing. He checked his watch and frowned. Andrew was a stickler for turning lights off, and for regular bedtimes. Something must have happened.

His first thought was for Tam. Had something happened? She was so far away. He couldn't bear it if . . .

Jumping from the car, he raced up to the front door and flung it open.

Something was wrong, all right. Moira was waiting for him just inside the door, wringing her hands together in despair.

'Oh, Matt,' she cried. 'Thank goodness. I don't know what to do.'

'Okay, love,' he said, putting his arm around her. 'What's wrong?'

'It's Andrew,' she wailed. 'You've got to do something. He won't let me call an ambulance . . . and I'm so sorry about your carpet.'

Moira wasn't the sort of woman to fall apart easily. Andrew was the worrier in that relationship. Moira was the calm one, as a rule. Gently he moved her to one side and hurried through to the lounge where he found Andrew sprawled on the sofa as if he'd been thrown there, his face grey.

'He'd just brought the coffee in when he collapsed. I'd just put the phone down and as I turned round, he was on the floor. The tray fell — there's coffee all over the carpet. I got him to the sofa and I tried to clear up the mess, but

— oh, Matt, I didn't know what to do. He's really ill, isn't he?'

Her hands were fluttering like birds and Matt took hold of them and held them still. 'Easy now,' he said. 'I'm here. I'll take over.'

He looked into her eyes. He'd never noticed before how alike Moira and Tam were. They both had those soft, gentle, grey eyes. He vaguely recalled Tam's mother, there had been nothing soft or gentle about her.

Matt looked at the mess on the floor and at the dark stain on the front of Andrew's shirt.

'That's not just spilt coffee, is it?' he said.

'Stop fussing,' Andrew said, his voice strained. 'It's nothing. Just a bit of indigestion. I probably scratched my throat when I vomited, that's all.'

'How long have you had this indigestion, Andrew?' Matt asked as he opened his bag.

'Too long,' Andrew muttered.

'Ulcer?'

'Probably.'

'Probably?' Matt repeated incredulously. How could Andrew be so stupid as to ignore these symptoms — to let things get this bad?

He felt angry. Angry because he loved this wretched man with all his heart. He loved him like a father because Andrew had always been the man that Matt's own mostly absent father could never be.

He was his role model, his inspiration and now he was sitting here in acute pain because he was too damn stubborn to see a doctor. Matt tried to forget how much he loved this man and carried on with his examination.

'Leave me alone,' Andrew snapped, trying weakly to push him away.

Matt took a firm hold of Andrew's wrist and felt an unpleasant thrill of dread shoot through his stomach. Andrew's pulse was rapid and weak, his skin clammy and cold.

'I'm going to call an ambulance and you are going to hospital.'

Andrew started to argue, but Matt silenced him.

'I'm not going to sit by and watch Moira made a widow because you're too stubborn to admit you're ill,' he said.

Moira looked from one to the other, her face more and more alarmed.

'Moira,' Matt said as he picked up the phone. 'Andrew has a stomach ulcer. I suspect that it's perforated. He's going to need emergency surgery.'

He broke off to make his ambulance request, then hung up and put his arms around Moira, who was shaking from head to foot. He was furious with Andrew for letting things go this far, for putting Moira through this agony.

'Oh, not another one,' she sobbed. 'Oh, please God, not another one.'

'Another one?' Matt frowned. 'Has Andrew had this before?'

'Oh!' Moira's hands flew to her face. 'No. That's not what I meant at all. I don't know what I'm saying. It's just

. . . he will be all right, won't he, Matt?'

'I'm sure he will,' he answered. 'But we'd better get hold of Jack. I'll try his mobile.' He glanced at Andrew. 'And maybe we should let Tam know as well,' he added.

'I'll do that,' Moira said. Suddenly she seemed to come to her senses. She ran her fingers through her hair and wiped her tears. 'I'll speak to her.'

'Well, I certainly hope you have better luck getting hold of her than I have,' Matt murmured.

'She just needs time,' Moira said distractedly.

What did she mean by that? It was as if she knew something he didn't.

'Perhaps you should think again about going to Australia,' Moira added.

'There's no question about it,' he said gravely. 'I'm going nowhere until Andrew is fit and well again. You're going to need me here now.'

* * *

'What is it with this family?' Matt said when Jack strolled into the surgery the next morning. 'You all seem to have a habit of vanishing off the face of the earth. I've been trying to get hold of you all night. Don't you ever turn your mobile phone on?'

Jack grinned. 'I was with a lady,' he drawled as he gave Matt a lazy smile. 'Leaving my phone on would have been rude.'

'Well, while you were with your *lady*, your father . . . ' Matt broke off. This wasn't the way to do it at all. He was angry with himself now. Had he really been about to break this news so heartlessly?

Jack's smile froze. 'What about my father?'

'He's all right,' Matt said quickly. 'I'm sorry, Jack. It's been a long night. Your father is in hospital. He had emergency surgery for a perforated ulcer.'

Unexpectedly, Jack crumpled. Matt quickly helped him to a chair.

'I'd seen the old fool popping pills,' Jack groaned. 'He told me they were breath mints. How could I be so stupid? Why didn't I see the signs?'

'None of us did, Jack,' Matt reassured him.

'What about Mum?'

'She's at the hospital. I brought her home so she could pick up some things and change her clothes, but she went straight back.'

Jack nodded. 'I should be there. But what about you, Matt? You're supposed to be leaving for Australia in a few days.'

'I've cancelled my plans,' Matt said stiffly.

Besides, he was pretty sure that once she knew what had happened, Tam would be on the next plane home. She loved Andrew as much as he did — and he knew very well that if he was on the other side of the world, wild horses wouldn't stop him coming back home at a time like this.

'We'll keep the locum on and he can

take Andrew's place rather than mine,' he went on.

As he watched Jack hurry back out to his car, Matt's thoughts turned again to Tam. He absolutely ached for her, but he wouldn't have wished for something like this to happen to bring her home.

Had he come on too strong and frightened her off? Was that it? Well, if she wanted a bit of time, then he'd give it to her. All the time in the world — because he'd wait forever if she asked him to.

2

Tam felt a terrific rush of emotion as she joined the coast road and saw a sight as familiar to her as her own hand.

I'm home, she thought. Almost a year had passed since she had left England for her Australian adventure. And what a year it had been.

First there had been the ectopic pregnancy, then that severe postoperative infection that had hospitalised her for weeks and more or less put an end to the slim hope that she might still be able to bear children. The last few months she'd spent gradually easing herself back into a proper working routine — and then suddenly it was time to come home.

A brisk wind was hurling clouds across the sky and whipping up foam on the waves, and she could taste the tang of salt on her lips.

Many years ago, she'd ridden a bike up this hill, her wheels kicking up a mixture of sand and dust in the dry summer heat, standing up to give more force to her strong tanned legs as they pumped up and down.

But Jack, four years older, had longer, stronger legs and had always left her behind, ignoring her shrieks of protest.

Of course, there had been Matt, who never left her behind. There was no escaping him. He was there, in her memories — as well as in her heart.

Matt's father had worked for the Foreign Office and spent so long out of the country, that sometimes Matt wouldn't see his parents for a year at a time. And as he grew up, he wanted to be a doctor like Andrew, not a diplomat like his father.

Matt had endless patience with Tam in those days, helping her catch fish in the rock pools and catching crabs off the old pier.

It had been her secret that while she

adored Jack like a big brother, her feelings for Matt were far different. She'd had a huge crush on him, which had made her behave foolishly around him at times, teasing him just so that he'd chase her.

But he wouldn't be chasing her any more. The last year had ended any hope she might have had of a future with Matt. She'd blown it. And now he'd left the practice. Aunt Moira hadn't said so, because she tended not to mention Matt in any of their conversations, but she did say that Tam was needed at home because they were one doctor short.

Aware that she could barely see the road through a sudden blur of tears, Tam pulled in at the side and switched off the engine.

She rubbed away her tears and pushed open the door, stepping outside into the gathering wind, gulping in the bracing salty sea air and listening to the mournful cry of the soaring gulls.

Matt had been a tall, skinny boy with

a scattering of freckles across his nose and a wonderful laugh. The freckles had long gone and he'd grown into a strong, handsome man — and even now when she thought of his laughter, it made her smile.

She was still smiling a little as she looked down at the beach below and spotted a lone figure on the sand.

A little early in the year to be swimming, she thought as the person below looked up, then stepped purposefully into the water. And then it hit her. People don't go swimming on cold March days.

'Hey,' she yelled. 'Hey, you down there.'

Her voice was snatched away by the wind, but she was already running towards the uneven path that wound down to the beach, her feet slipping on loose stones.

Cara's last words to her, warning her to take things easy and not to forget how ill she'd been, were forgotten.

Several times, she almost lost her

footing, but she carried on running.

Halfway down, she had another look. It was a woman with long blonde hair and she was waist deep in the water, the waves hitting her chest, almost knocking her down. It must have been freezing.

'Oh, please,' Tam murmured as she negotiated the last section of the path. The woman was now up to her chest, falling forward into the waves with her arms outstretched, allowing the sea to take her.

'No!' Tam screamed.

She ran, slipped and fell, scraping her leg on one of the rocks, smashing her knee as she landed.

Scrambling back to her feet, grazing her hands on the rocks as she used them to help her up, she broke into a run again. All she could see of the woman was her head bobbing in the water, the strong current already sweeping her away.

At last, her feet hit the wet sand and she was able to move faster, ignoring the pain in her knee and the throbbing ache in her chest as she slammed her feet down between the scattered rocks.

The water wrapped round her legs like icy claws as she ran into it. The cold took her breath away, but she had to keep going.

Only as she plunged into the choppy sea and began to swim into the waves did she realise what a stupid thing she was doing. Before embarking on this rescue mission, she should at least have phoned to summon help.

One of the waves went over her head; salt water filled her mouth and burned her nostrils. She had to reach that poor woman, had to save her — because, whatever terrible thing had driven her to such a desperate act, nothing was worth losing your life for.

At last she saw the woman's head just above the water. She wasn't giving herself to the sea so readily now and was struggling, and splashing hopelessly in an effort to stay afloat. Tam realised with a sinking heart that this foolhardy rescue attempt was going to be anything but easy.

* * *

The red motorcycle swerved in behind the apparently abandoned car and its rider frowned behind the darkened visor of his black crash helmet.

The car following him up the hill also stopped, its driver climbing out and joining him. Adrian York was the new partner who had originally been the locum who stood in for Tam.

'Who'd leave a car like that, with the driver's door wide open?' he said.

'Just what I was asking myself,' Matt said as he climbed off his motorbike and wrenched the helmet off his head. 'We'd better take a look.' He strode over to the car and leaned on the roof, looking first inside, then down at the beach. His unease increased.

He turned to the sea and saw two people in the water some distance from the shore and realised at once what was happening.

He called to Adrian, 'Have you got your phone?'

'Yes. Why, what's going on? Someone hurt?'

'There are two people in difficulty out there. Call for help, then follow me down to the harbour. We can both go out on the lifeboat.'

He sped down to the little harbour, his heart pounding. In a situation like this, every second counted; every passing moment could mean the difference between life and death.

Volunteers were running from all parts of the small coastal town, having dropped whatever they were doing to join the rescue. Within minutes, the inshore lifeboat was launched. Matt just hoped they'd be in time.

* * *

'Hold still,' Tam shouted at the squirming, kicking woman she was trying desperately to rescue. 'I'm trying to help you.'

'Leave me alone,' the woman screamed back at her, lashing out with hands that had little strength left. 'I want to die.'

As Tam tried to help her, the woman pushed her under the water. Tam surfaced, gulping for air, the salt water stinging her eyes.

No sooner had she recovered from that than a wave engulfed them both, catching Tam by surprise. She swallowed yet more salt water, felt it burn all the way down to her stomach.

Glancing back, she realised the current had already dragged them a long way from the shore.

'I won't let you die,' Tam said, reaching out and grasping the woman around the shoulders.

'I want to die,' she said and suddenly, she was sobbing with heartbreaking desperation as her body went limp against Tam's. 'It's all gone wrong. There's nothing to live for.'

'Maybe not now,' Tam gasped. 'But there will be. Please, trust me. I need you to help me if we're to make it back to the beach.'

She was so cold now that her teeth were chattering. She wasn't even sure they'd make it back. It was no consolation knowing she'd done her best. After all she'd been through this past year, she hadn't come home only to drown before she'd even said hello to her aunt and uncle.

That thought gave her renewed strength but, to her horror, the woman in her arms lost consciousness. She'd be no help at all now. Tam was completely on her own.

And she was growing colder and colder. Her only chance would be to let the woman go, allow her to slide under the water where she wanted to be. Then, maybe, she'd have the strength to get herself back to the safety of the beach. But Tam couldn't do that. She'd save this woman, whoever she was, or die trying.

Numbness crept up her legs and her hands were almost gleaming white. She knew only too well that the cold was impairing her swimming ability. But she would probably drown before hypothermia set in. The woman in her arms was another matter. She'd stopped shivering and her breathing was shallow, her pulse fading. If help didn't arrive soon, she would die.

'Someone, help us,' Tam shouted. She knew it was useless and that she should conserve her energy.

Then she heard it. The thrum of the inshore lifeboat. At least she wasn't shivering now — and while a part of her acknowledged that this may not necessarily be a good sign, another part was relieved.

The woman she'd saved was pulled from her arms and drawn into the safe cocoon of the boat, then strong arms were reaching out for her. All she could think of at that moment was how striking her rescuer's blue eyes were in his rugged face. Intense blue eyes, just like . . .

Suddenly the swell increased and Tam went under. As she tried to kick her way back to the surface, her foot hit the rocks a few feet down and she was caught, her foot wedged between two rocks.

She struggled to free herself, but nothing happened and she was too exhausted and cold to carry on. She was caught fast. And her lungs felt as if they were about to burst. She hadn't even had time to gulp in some air before she went under.

Suddenly hands reached out for her, moved down her body, found her trapped foot. She clung to her rescuer as he twisted and tugged on her foot, then she was free and breaking the surface again, gulping lungfuls of air.

Gasping, unable to see for the salt in her eyes, she felt more hands reaching for her, hauling her aboard the boat.

Her rescuer pushed from behind, then climbed up behind her. He turned her over and she heard him exclaim.

'Adrian — can you take care of her? I'll see to Sally.'

Sally, Tam thought distantly. *There's a coincidence. Didn't Moira mention Jack had a girlfriend called Sally*?

'Hi, I'm Adrian,' another man said. 'You're safe now.'

Tam tried to smile, but her eyes felt so heavy and when she tried to speak, she gagged violently.

Matt felt dazed. It was bad enough finding out that Sally had tried to drown herself, without coming face to face with Tam — and then almost immediately losing her as she was sucked back under.

One moment he'd had her in his hands, and the next she'd gone. The split second that she was under the water, when he realised she should have come back to the surface, had seemed to last forever.

Freeing her from the rocks had taken a lifetime, with precious seconds ticking past when he'd worried that she may not be able to hold her breath, may be too weak and exhausted to even try. Then when they surfaced, she didn't seem to recognise him at all. But did he expect her to? She was choking and gagging when he handed her over to Adrian.

If he'd thought he was over her, then he'd been kidding himself. She seemed smaller than he remembered, almost frail — and there wasn't the hint of a tan, considering she'd spent the past year in Australia.

He busied himself looking after Sally, but his heart was elsewhere on the boat. Battered and bruised though it was, his heart still responded crazily to Tamara Lawrence.

He'd known she was coming back, of course. No sooner had Jack done his vanishing act than Moira said, oh so casually, that Tam was coming home to replace him.

No one had bothered to ask him his opinion, of course. They'd just assumed he'd be as delighted as they were that she was coming back. At first he'd felt like following Jack to Thailand, or wherever it was that he'd gone this time, but then he'd thought: why should he?

Tam was just as likely to get fed up in a few months and take off again. Just like his parents. The pattern was all too familiar. Love and promises, followed by disappointment. Apart from Moira and Andrew, Matt couldn't think of a single person in his life who hadn't let him down.

Back on shore, he handed care of both women over to the waiting paramedics, but he hung around outside Tam's ambulance, listening shamelessly at the open doors, telling himself his interest was purely professional.

'I'm fine, really,' Tam protested as she sat in the ambulance being checked over by a paramedic. 'There's no need for me to go to hospital.'

'The doctor wants you checked out at the hospital,' the paramedic said. 'Be a good girl and do as you're told.'

'Don't patronise me,' she said irritably. 'All I was doing was trying to save that woman.'

'That's a symptom of hypothermia,' the paramedic grinned. 'Being irritable.'

'I'm not . . . ' she stopped, took a deep breath and smiled. 'I promise you, I'm fine. I'm a doctor, I know what I'm talking about.'

'Then you'll know that if salt water has got into your lungs, you're at risk of cardiac arrest. And of course you'll have heard of secondary drowning — '

'I can't leave my car! It isn't locked, and practically everything I own is in it,' Tam cried. She tried to move, but was held back by wires and an oxygen mask which the paramedic kept trying, unsuccessfully, to make her wear. She tore it from her face and tried to glare at him, but it was such a friendly face that smiled back at her, that she slumped back, defeated.

There was a rustling noise outside and the paramedic turned to look.

'Matt, did you want to take a look at her?'

Matt? Those incredible blue eyes. Tam suddenly realised exactly who had pulled her out of the water. She hadn't been imagining things after all. Her heart began to thump and embarrassingly, the monitor reflected the sudden burst of activity.

Tam looked round, saw Matt stepping up into the back of the ambulance and couldn't catch her breath for a moment. She'd forgotten just how tall, strong and powerful he was, but she hadn't forgotten how he made her feel.

The last time she'd looked into that face, he'd just kissed her goodbye before she boarded her flight to Sydney. His eyes, then so full of longing, were now cold and impassive. Expressionless. As if he felt absolutely nothing for her.

She smiled weakly, but he either didn't see or chose to ignore it.

His dark damp hair clung to his face and neck. Moisture trickled from his hair down his cheeks.

Oh, Matt, she thought, *I still love you*.

He checked the monitor then looked into her eyes very briefly before turning back to the monitor.

'Matt . . . ' she whispered.

'I'm afraid you can't go home just yet,' he said. 'You're going to have to stay in hospital for a while. That nasty gash on your leg will need treatment.'

Tam stared at him and blinked. What was he doing? His voice was flat as he spoke to her. There was no emotion there at all. It was almost as if he didn't know her. But what did she expect? A warm welcome?

'I'll see that your car is moved,' he went on, still managing not to look at her. 'It was a very brave thing you did. Not to mention very stupid.'

'I know,' she said, closing her eyes so that she didn't have to look at him not looking at her. 'But in circumstances like that, you don't always do the sensible thing.'

When she opened her eyes again, he'd gone.

'I thought he'd left the practice,' she said.

'It's Jack Carter that's gone,' the paramedic said.

So it was Jack she was coming home to replace — not Matt at all. Aunt Moira had tricked her. There had been no need for tricks. After all, where else would she have gone when she came back? Knowing that her aunt and uncle and Heron Bay were here had got her through this last year.

'I'm Jack's cousin,' she said heavily. 'I'm replacing him at Bay House.'

'So you really are a doctor.'

'Did you doubt me?'

'You have been rambling a bit.'

The ambulance set off. All Tam could think about was working alongside Matt. It was completely unexpected and she didn't know how she'd cope.

One thing was for sure. She wasn't going to have to worry about keeping

Matt at a distance. He seemed quite happy to distance himself.

* * *

Matt sat in Tam's car for a long while looking out over Heron Bay. Why had she come back? Why now? After the way she'd behaved, he was amazed that she had the gall.

It wasn't just the fact that she'd suddenly backed out of their blossoming relationship; it was the way she'd done it. Through her aunt, for heaven's sake. He had to hear it from Moira.

Had Tam any notion at all of how humiliating that had been? She was more like Jack than he'd given her credit for.

He thought of Sally. The poor kid, driven to try and drown herself because of Jack. He hadn't just cut and run — he'd cut and run off with someone else, or so the rumour mill had it. He wondered if that's how it had been for Tam. Had she met some bronzed Australian surfer?

He suddenly realised he was in great danger of turning into a self-pitying idiot. There were far worse things that could happen to a person than having their heart broken, far worse. He saw them in his surgery every week.

He thrust the key into the ignition and started the engine, pressing down hard on the accelerator.

3

Much later, Tam woke up from a deep sleep. It took a while for her to find her bearings. She was in a hospital bed and, for a moment, she almost panicked, thinking herself back in Australia, back in hospital.

But apart from a knot of pain in her knee, a sore leg and a burning throat, she felt fine.

She turned and saw a cloud of white hair beside the bed. It belonged to a visitor who had nodded off herself. Tam choked back her tears and reached out a hand. 'Aunt Moira?'

The older woman woke with a start, then sat up straight and smiled at Tam. 'Oh! You're awake, dear.' Moira got up and leaned over to kiss Tam's cheek. 'I wanted to be here when you woke up. How are you feeling?'

'All the better, seeing you.' Tam

smiled as the threatening tears receded.

Moira's eyes welled with tears now as she searched Tam's face, looking over every inch of it.

'If you knew how much I wanted to jump on a plane and come and drag you home,' she said. 'You've been through so much — and now you've come back and straight away saved Sally's life. She's going to be all right, thanks to you.'

Tam realised that her rescue had the potential to become very embarrassing. 'Anyone would have done the same,' she said. 'Except someone else might have had the sense to call for help before leaping in.'

'Well that's you all over,' Moira smiled. 'Impulsive. You were just the same as a child.'

Tam reached for her aunt's hand and gave it a squeeze.

'I'm so sorry, Aunt Moira,' she said. 'What on earth made Jack take off like that?'

'Who knows?' Moira shrugged. 'I

gather Sally was just getting too serious, and you know Jack — he's never serious. It means we're rather stuck with Sally. She's a nice enough girl, but she doesn't seem to want to move on I'm afraid.' She sighed, then perked up. 'Goodness knows where your uncle has gone. He wandered off to see a couple of his patients. You know what he's like. He's supposed to be semi-retired, but you'd never believe it, the hours he puts in. Oh, I can't tell you how good it is to have you back here again.'

She grabbed a tissue from the box on the locker and dabbed at her eyes.

'Just like old times, except . . . '

'Except Jack isn't here.' Tam smiled gently.

Moira nodded. 'They're going to keep you in tonight and I'm going to come and collect you in the morning. Now you must get as much rest as you can, my dear. If I find your uncle, I'll get him to come and say goodnight.'

She bent over and kissed Tam's cheek.

'What about Matt?' Tam asked. 'How has he been? I really thought he was the one who'd left.'

'I'm afraid that's what I let you think,' Moira admitted. 'I thought if you knew Matt was still here, you might not come back. I'm so glad you're here.'

'So am I,' Tam replied.

'I did as you asked and I didn't tell a soul about how ill you were, not even Andrew. I was tempted to tell Matt when Cara rang and told me about that dreadful infection you got, but there never really was a right moment.'

'Thank you, Aunt Moira,' Tam said, squeezing her aunt's hands. 'There's no need for anyone to know what happened.'

Moira's face said that she didn't believe that for one moment, but she simply said, 'Welcome home.'

As Tam watched Moira walk away, a wave of sadness washed over her. Her aunt seemed to have aged so suddenly. She'd always been such a vital, attractive woman, but now she looked thin and strained.

Did I do that to her? Tam wondered. Was it all the worry about her, topped off by Jack walking out?

'How are you feeling?'

She gave a start, realising Matt was approaching from the other end of the ward. Her heart leapt at the sight of him.

He was wearing a leather jacket and faded blue jeans tucked into black leather boots. A black crash helmet hung from one hand, and he looked more like a biker than a doctor. He looked good. Better than good.

'You have a motorbike?' She couldn't disguise her surprise. Matt had always been a very reserved and conventional person.

He picked up her chart and once again managed to avoid looking at her. *How long is this going to go on?* Tam wondered. *How long can we avoid looking at each other?*

'Ducati. Bought it a few months ago,'

he said, still without looking up.

Jack was about motorbikes and reckless living, not Matt.

'I was just thinking how frail my aunt looks,' she said, cursing the shake in her voice.

'Jack going like he did really knocked her for six,' Matt said. 'That and all the worry. She's had a lousy year one way and another and frankly, I'm surprised you haven't been back sooner to offer your support.'

Tam felt stung by the harsh accusation in his voice. What right did he have to judge her? She looked the other way quickly so he wouldn't see the hurt in her eyes. What did he mean about Moira having a lousy year? Had she told him about Tam, despite her assurances to the contrary?

'Sally's going to be fine,' he went on, still studying the notes with more intensity than was necessary. 'Well, as fine as the poor girl can be after all she's been through. You saved her life. If I hadn't seen your car there and stopped to see what was going on, she'd have been swept out to sea — and you with her.'

He was treating her like a stranger — as if they had never been childhood friends, let alone lovers.

'Thank you . . . ' A flicker of a smile crossed his face and she felt warmed until she realised the smile wasn't for her.

'Well, this is a sight for sore eyes.' Andrew Carter's deep voice rang out. 'You were sleeping like a baby last time I looked at you.'

'Uncle Andrew!' Tam cried as she tried desperately to hide her shock. Gone was the big, broad man who had once owned that voice and in his place was a thin, almost shadowy figure.

His hair, just a year ago so thick and bushy, had thinned and his eyes were sunken. There was more than Jack's leaving behind this sudden change — much more. There had to be.

Andrew lifted both her hands in his and looked into her eyes.

'I'm so sorry about all of this,' he said. 'I know you planned to join us eventually, but you rushed back to replace Jack and this had to happen.'

She glanced at Matt and realised that he too was looking at Andrew with some concern. What had been going on here?

'I think I'll be off, Andrew,' Matt said. 'Take care, now, and I'll see you in the morning.'

'Thank you, Matt,' Andrew said. 'For everything.'

Matt placed his hand on Andrew's shoulder and gave it a gentle squeeze. 'Any time,' he said, his deep affection for the older man clear in his voice. 'You know that.'

He turned and caught Tam's eye. For a moment she thought she saw a flicker of the old affection there, but he gave a curt nod and turned away.

Her heart felt heavy as she watched Matt stride out of the ward. Her sense of loss was deepening with every passing moment.

'He's as dear as . . . ' Andrew began, then his eyes narrowed with pain and he shook his head. 'I was going to say as a son, but that would sound rather like an insult after the way Jack has behaved.'

'Of course it wouldn't,' Tam said, squeezing his hands.

'And you, of course, are as dear as a daughter,' he said, his smile back in place. 'But that goes without saying. Now, I've had my instructions from Moira not to keep you chatting and to let you rest. So I'll be away back to Bay House for now and all being well, we'll see you there tomorrow.'

'You've lost weight since you've been away,' he said frowning. 'I know you had a dunking, but that doesn't explain the shadows under your eyes. And you're so pale. What happened to that Australian sunshine?'

'I'm fine,' she assured him as he kissed her goodnight.

Tam felt intensely sad as she watched him go, just as she'd felt so sad earlier watching Moira. There was a slight stoop to his shoulders and he no longer stepped out with confidence.

* * *

If her leg had been painful yesterday, it was nothing to how it felt today. Tam bit her lip and winced as she tested her weight on it. The duty doctor had seen her and declared her fit to be discharged, and all she had to do was wait for Aunt Moira to pick her up.

She hadn't any make-up with her, and when she looked in the mirror she had a shock. Her face was deathly pale, and her grey eyes were washed out and rimmed with dark shadows.

It was Matt who walked into the ward at just after nine o'clock and Tam felt her stomach sink.

He was wearing the leather jacket again over a white shirt and black trousers and this time he wasn't carrying his crash helmet.

'How are you this morning?' he

asked, more formal than friendly.

'Keen to get home,' she said.

He made no comment on her appearance, but then he didn't look at her long enough to take anything about her on board.

'I'm sorry I'm late,' he murmured as he picked up the small paper bag containing the antibiotics and ointment the ward sister had given her. 'I stopped by to see Sally. They're keeping her in for a few more hours.'

'Are you taking me home?'

'Do you have a problem with that?' He raised an enquiring eyebrow.

It hit her then in a rush. He'd changed. He didn't even look the same. He was no less attractive and could still make her heart leap, but he was cold.

'I was expecting Aunt Moira, that's all. Is everything all right?'

He gave her a long look that made her skin tingle. She'd wanted him to look at her, but now he was doing it, it was she who turned abruptly away.

'Everything is fine,' he said at last.

'Are you ready?'

'Yes. Look, I can call a taxi if you'd prefer.'

He gave her another of those unnerving looks and when he spoke his voice was softer. 'No need. But we can't hang about. We're a doctor short and there's a lot to do.'

'I thought that was why I was here,' she said.

'And we can't wait to have you start work,' Matt said agreeably, as if talking to a stranger. 'But I want you fully fit, which means a few days' rest.'

'I'll be ready to start work tomorrow,' Tam insisted. 'That's when I was due to take my first surgery. It's what I agreed with Uncle Andrew.'

'Still as stubborn as ever,' Matt said.

'And you're still as bossy,' she replied with a smile which, to her delight, he returned.

As they set off walking, he saw at once that she was in some discomfort. He held out his arm. 'Hang on to me,' he said.

'No, I . . . '

'Just hold my arm, Tam,' he said impatiently.

Her face flamed, but she slipped her arm through his and thanked him.

'I said, *hang on to me*,' he said. 'I could still hoist you over my shoulder and run with you if I wanted to.'

Laughing, she held on a little tighter and felt the soft leather of his jacket brush her cheek. She was more pleased than she liked to admit, even to herself, that he remembered those far-off summer days and what's more, seemed to recall them with some affection. She leaned in to him.

'I'll just say goodbye to the nursing staff before we leave.'

'They'll probably be glad to see the back of you,' Matt said. 'They say doctors are the worst patients. I've never known one worse than Andrew.'

Tam looked up sharply and stopped in her tracks.

'I knew it,' she said. 'What's wrong with him, Matt? How serious is it?

More to the point, why didn't anyone tell me?'

Matt sighed heavily. 'Do you really expect me to believe that you don't have a clue about what's been going on here?'

'Apart from being able to see for myself that he's unwell, no,' she said. 'I don't have the faintest idea. I hope you're going to put me in the picture.'

She looked awful, with those big black rings round her eyes, as if she was on her way to a Hallowe'en party. And she'd *shrunk*.

It didn't suit her — but, instead of making her less attractive, it just brought all sorts of unwanted feelings rushing to the fore — not least that he wanted to hold her. It was going to be difficult, but not impossible, to carry on as if nothing had happened between them last year.

He was still feeling shaken by her surprise about Andrew. How could she not know? Moira had said, more than once, that Tam was fully aware of what was happening at home. She'd also told him that he wasn't to call Tam or write to her; that she needed space.

Space? She was thousands of miles away. How much space did she need, for heaven's sake?

Could Moira have lied to him, too? He frowned as they made their slow way across the car park. Moira hadn't exactly lied to Tam. It seemed she'd just omitted to tell her the truth. Had she done the same to him?

'Are you all right, Matt?'

'Sorry.' He smiled quickly. 'Miles away. Here we are. This is my car.'

He pointed his key at a silver BMW convertible and heard Tam's sharp intake of breath. He smiled again. It gave him a certain sense of satisfaction to surprise her. Indeed, he'd surprised himself this past year.

Matt opened the car door and held it while Tam got in, making sure she was settled before closing the door. She watched him walk round the front of the car, staring at the strands of his dark hair curling against his strong neck, and shivered.

So what had happened in the past year? More than Jack running off, that much was certain.

As for this car — It was a Jack kind of car.

Matt drove out of the car park and turned towards Heron Bay, his face set, his eyes seeming to look somewhere beyond the road ahead.

After a few minutes silence, Tam couldn't wait any longer. 'You were going to tell me about Uncle Andrew,' she reminded him gently.

His shoulders dropped, his hands loosened their grip on the steering wheel and he let out a long breath.

'It's not my place to tell you, but equally it was wrong of Moira and Andrew to keep you in the dark. Moira told me that she'd let you know. Do you know anything at all about what's been happening here since you left?'

'Nothing,' she admitted. 'I rang Aunt Moira as often as I could and she never gave as much as a hint that anything was wrong. She didn't even tell me about Jack running out on Sally.'

'I see,' Matt said.

She waited while he seemed to consider what he was going to say.

'They were always so protective over you, Tam,' he said, keeping his eyes fixed on the road ahead. 'If only Moira and Andrew had known what you were really like.'

'What I was really like?' Tam whispered.

'You know what I mean. If there was trouble to get into. You got into it,' Matt said, his eyes twinkling as if the memories weren't exactly bad ones. 'I lost count of the times Jack and I had to get you out of scrapes. But Jack was almost as bad.' The last sentence was said with a wistful air.

'And Jack got worse.'

A muscle twitched in his cheek and the humour vanished from his eyes.

'A lot worse, especially this past year. And I just don't understand why. He had everything. Sally, a secure future, a great home . . . '

'Unlike you,' Tam whispered softly.

'Jack's a damn fool. He couldn't see how lucky he was. To be honest with you, Tam, by the time he left I didn't even like him much any more.'

'That doesn't sound like the Jack I knew,' Tam said, feeling she should defend her cousin.

'Then perhaps you didn't know him as well as you thought,' Matt said and lapsed into silence again.

Tam struggled to find something to say, anything, but all she could do was look at him with a kind of pained desperation. Had he any notion, could he possibly know, just how much she loved him?

She could almost feel the excitement she'd felt as a child, coming up this hill in her uncle's car at the beginning of summer. And in her mind, she could see Matt and Jack waiting at the top of the hill, sitting astride their bikes watching out for her.

She opened her eyes and realised Matt was slowing down and pulling over in almost the same spot that she'd pulled in yesterday.

'Beautiful, isn't it?' he said without looking at her. 'All my good memories are here.'

'Mine too,' she said hoarsely. 'Matt, tell me about Uncle Andrew.'

He turned to face her.

What if it was bad news? The worst? She wasn't sure she could face her aunt and uncle straight away if she knew.

'But perhaps not now,' she added quickly, knowing she was copping out. 'You said you had surgery . . . '

'I called Adrian from the hospital,' Matt answered. 'He's seeing my patients this morning. We have time to talk, if that's what you want. Shall we step outside?'

They got out of the car and immediately Tam felt the spring chill on her skin. But through the chill, she could feel the warmth of the sun.

She made her way unsteadily to the edge of the road and looked down at the beach.

Had she really rushed into that water yesterday? It felt unreal, as if it had happened to someone else and she'd been a bystander. And if Matt hadn't come along when he did . . .

He'd saved her life. It hit her with a jolt. If not for him, then she wouldn't be standing here at all.

'When we were kids, Jack and I used to wait at the top of the hill for you to appear,' Matt said and she turned to look at him. He was leaning back against his car, arms folded, the wind ruffling his dark hair.

'That's funny,' she said. 'I was thinking of exactly that when you stopped the car.'

'You remember it?' He looked ridiculously pleased.

'Of course I do. It was all part of the fun, seeing you and Jack.'

To her surprise he laughed softly.

'I used to worry that you wouldn't be

on the train, or that something had happened to you,' he said. 'Then the car would come round the corner at the bottom of the hill and as it drew closer, I'd just see your little white face peeping above the dashboard.'

This was a revelation. Tam thought her cousin and Matt used to see her as a nuisance to be tolerated all summer. Never in her wildest dreams did she imagine Matt might actually look forward to her arrival. She certainly didn't know he worried about her.

'You used to worry about me?'

He shrugged. 'You were just a little kid. I was used to being stuck on trains and planes on my own, but you seemed so small and vulnerable.'

'Me?' she murmured.

'Why so surprised? You were quite a bit younger than me and I felt responsible. It was always me Moira asked to watch out for you, not Jack.'

She laughed suddenly. 'I could take on you boys any day,' she said defiantly. 'And win.'

'Only because we let you. And when we used to go out in the boat or go fishing on the pier, I was terrified you'd fall in. I know you were a strong swimmer, but . . . And then yesterday it was as if all my childhood nightmares had suddenly become real. There you were in my hands, and suddenly you were torn away from me. I thought . . . ' he hesitated. 'I thought I'd lost you.'

His voice was ragged and the laughter had gone from his eyes.

'I thought so too,' she said soberly, then she turned away from him again, thrust her hands in her pockets and looked out across the sea before he'd have time to read the expression on her face. She bit hard on her lip.

Stupid wobbly lip, she thought angrily. He was speaking again, and this time his voice was steady and firm.

'Then by the end of the summer, you were brown and bright and your hair would be bleached almost white by the sun. It was as if you came alive here. As if we all did. The part of my childhood spent here with your aunt and uncle were my salvation. And you were part of that.'

She couldn't speak; couldn't turn back to face him. If only she hadn't hurt her damned leg, she'd suggest he drove the rest of the way and leave her to walk home. Right now she needed to be as far away from him as possible before she did something really stupid.

All she wanted was to tell him how much she loved him. She wanted to tell him about the child they had made together and she'd lost, and yet she knew that could never be. She gulped in the bracing air, hoping to clear her head of such wild thoughts.

Then she heard a sound behind her and when she finally turned round, she saw he'd got back in the car and was sitting staring at the road ahead.

She couldn't keep running away from this. She had to find out what had happened to change Andrew and Moira so much — and if it was bad, then she'd just have to get on with it and cope. It was time to stop thinking about herself and start thinking about Moira and how she could help her.

4

How much harder was this going to get? Matt had taken two steps towards her and was ready to crush her in his arms before he suddenly came to his senses.

If she'd seemed small and pale and vulnerable as a kid, then it was nothing to how she seemed to him now. Smaller than ever, paler than ever and with such an air of fragility about her that everything in him wanted to protect and care for her.

And love her.

Oh God, how everything in him ached to love her.

Two steps, then he'd turned abruptly and got back in the car. If she'd turned around before he'd managed that, then God knows what would have happened.

He could have declared his undying love for her — and then what? Would she have laughed in his face? Pushed him away? That would have been even harder to bear. She'd rejected him once and he'd survived. He wasn't sure if he could do it again.

I thought I'd lost you. Had he really said that? Idiot!

He dragged his gaze away from the road and looked at her. She was facing the car now, staring at him with those huge bleak grey eyes of hers. If he didn't know better, he'd think she was confused and perhaps a little afraid. He might even think she'd been ill — quite apart from the events of the day before. But he did know better.

He opened the car window and said more harshly than he intended, 'You'd better get in. Moira will never forgive me if I let you get cold.'

He didn't look at her as she got in the car beside him and when she fumbled with her seat belt, he stopped himself from helping her. She wasn't his to care for. Not his responsibility and the sooner he got that through his skull, the better it would be for everyone.

'Matt,' she said.

He switched on the engine.

'We should have a talk,' she said urgently. 'Before we get to the house.'

'Talk?' He felt his shoulders stiffen.

'About Uncle Andrew.'

'Ah.' He switched off the engine again, relief flooding through him.

They were friends before all this happened. Good friends. They could be again, as long as he kept a tight rein on his emotions.

'And I haven't thanked you yet for saving my life,' she said. 'If it hadn't been for you — '

'Don't,' he said. 'I would have done the same for anyone. I'm a lifeboat man as well as a doctor. I could hardly have thrown you back.'

Tam wished he wouldn't keep looking at her like that. He was either avoiding eye contact altogether, or he was looking at her so deeply she felt as if he were trying to delve into her soul — or at the very least, to read her thoughts. But there was nothing to see. They'd had a fling. Yes, that's what she'd decided to call it. A fling. It happened a long time ago, they were both grown-ups and it was now time to move on.

'Andrew had to undergo emergency surgery last year,' Matt explained. 'For a perforated ulcer.'

Tam swallowed hard. 'I thought . . . maybe it was cancer,' she said. 'Was it just an ulcer?'

She was wringing her hands in her lap, staring at them. The feeling that it might be something worse had been nagging at the back of her mind. If Matt had bad news to break, then she couldn't look at him while he did it, not without falling apart. It was vital that she held it together from now on.

'*Just* an ulcer?' Matt said incredulously. 'It very nearly killed him. Typically he ignored the symptoms for far too long and ended up having a partial gastrectomy.'

'My mother was a lot younger than

him when she died, Matt. It started with stomach pains she ignored, and by the time she sought help . . . ' She broke off. There was no need to go into all that now. 'Proper investigations were made, weren't they? There wasn't anything else . . . '

'No, love,' Matt said, his tone softening considerably. 'Nothing nasty lurking behind the scenes.'

She leaned back in the seat and let out her breath in a rush. 'Why didn't anyone tell me?'

'Moira said she had.'

Oh no. She didn't have to ask exactly when it had happened. She'd already guessed. While she was ill. And while she was burdening Moira with her own troubles, the poor woman was coping with a dangerously ill husband herself.

'She should have told me,' she murmured.

'Presumably she had her reasons not to,' Matt said. 'She saw your trip to Australia as your big chance. But if I'd known you weren't aware of what was going on here, I would have let you know. Somehow. Even though you wouldn't speak to me.'

'Matt, I'm sorry.'

She tried to look at him, but couldn't, fearing that the whole story would come rushing out before she could stop it.

'You had your reasons,' he said lightly, as if it really didn't matter.

'But he still looks so ill,' she said. 'Surely he should be looking better?'

'The stomach perforation dragged him down,' Matt said soberly. 'The heart attack two months later nearly finished the job.'

'Heart attack?' Tam felt as if she'd been punched.

'Believe me, Tam, he looks much better than he did a few months ago. Jack's leaving knocked him for six, but his recovery will speed along now that you're here to share the load. Moira and I are hoping to persuade him to retire fully. That's if you're planning on sticking around.'

Tam caught her lip between her teeth and bit down hard. Until yesterday there would have been no question about her staying. It had always been her dream to live and work in Heron Bay, and she'd come here with every intention of doing just that. But that was when she thought Matt was no longer on the scene.

If she upped sticks and ran away now, then she'd be no better than her cousin. She couldn't do it to them. And yet, and yet . . .

She looked up and realised that he was staring at her searchingly and she had the feeling he was asking a lot more than was in his question.

'Are you, Tam?'

'I-I don't know,' she said.

'Let's get you home,' he said. 'Moira will be waiting.'

He started the car again and they completed their journey to Bay House in silence. He pulled up outside the front door and before Tam could move, he was round her side of the car, holding the door open.

'All right?'

'Yes, thanks,' she said, smiling, so relieved to be home at last. She climbed out of the car and looked up at the familiar walls of the house, the morning sun reflecting in the windows.

Matt rested his hand lightly on her waist as she walked to the front door, there ready if she should stumble or feel the need to lean on him.

Whatever chemistry had existed between them before she went away was still there, and more so. She was going to have to fight it with every ounce of her strength.

'Let's get you inside,' he said gruffly.

'What kept you?' Moira greeted them in the hall. 'Is everything all right?'

'Everything's fine, Moira,' Matt said.

Moira held Tam's arms at her sides and looked deeply at her.

'I didn't realise . . . ' she began. 'When you were in the hospital bed, you didn't look . . . I mean, heavens, child, you've lost so much weight and you didn't have much there in the first place.'

Tam smiled. If Moira had seen her just a couple of months ago! She'd looked even worse then.

'I really wouldn't worry, Moira.' Matt jumped in to the rescue. 'She's been given a clean bill of health from the hospital and she must be made of pretty good stuff to have bounced back from all that drama yesterday.'

'Yes, but — ' Moira pressed her lips together, all too aware that she couldn't say too much in front of Matt. 'I don't want you overdoing things, now, Tam.'

'I won't, but Matt's right,' Tam said, hoping to reassure her aunt without giving anything away. 'I'm on the mend now, and a few weeks of your cooking and I'll be back to normal.'

'Of course you will,' Moira said. 'I've a meeting about the Sea Festival and then I'm going to pick Sally up. But I can cancel the meeting and cook lunch. It would just take a phone call.'

'You'll do no such thing,' Tam said. 'I'm fine, as you can see.'

'I can plainly see you are not,' Moira whispered under her breath.

'Adrian's covering for me,' Matt said calmly. 'You go to your meeting and I'll stay with Tam until you get back.'

'Bless you,' Moira said, then she cupped Tam's face in her hands. 'At least I know you're in safe hands with Matt. He'll take good care of you. Will you make lunch? I've left . . . '

'Go,' Matt said. 'I should know my way around your kitchen by now.'

As soon as Moira had gone, Tam turned to Matt. 'It's okay. You don't have to stay. I can manage quite well on my own and I expect you've got plenty to do.'

'Don't you want me to stay, Tam?' he asked.

'I just don't want you to feel . . . burdened.'

He laughed. 'Well, I didn't have time for breakfast this morning and I'm ravenous, so if you don't mind I'll rustle us up some lunch before I go anywhere else.'

He led the way to the kitchen and went straight to the fridge.

'Anything you fancy?'

'Actually, I am pretty hungry,' she admitted. 'I had no breakfast either.'

'How about pasta?'

'Pasta would be lovely.'

'As usual, Moira's fridge is well stocked with just about everything,' he said. 'I'll make a carbonara sauce and while I'm doing that, perhaps you can throw a salad together. How does that sound?'

'Wonderful,' she said. 'Where's Uncle Andrew?'

'In his surgery,' Matt said. 'He works every morning.'

They moved about the kitchen preparing lunch.

'When would you like to start work?' Matt asked as he stirred the sauce.

'Tomorrow.'

She was sitting at the big old table making the salad and he stood at the cooking range, keeping his back to her. He'd slung his leather jacket over the back of a chair, and she found herself staring at him.

She'd stopped chopping, her knife poised over a quartered apple, her gaze fixed on the back of his neck and her mind lost in her wistful thoughts.

He would have been such a good father. Our child would have been loved and cherished and not bundled onto a train every school holiday just to get him or her out of the way.

Tears began to threaten and she struggled to hold them back.

Her mother had been a lousy parent, yet somehow they had made their peace and during her mother's battle for life, they'd found the closeness that had always seemed to elude them. But for such a heartbreakingly short time. Her mother had wept and begged Tam's forgiveness for her shortcomings, and Tam told her there was nothing to forgive.

She wasn't bitter about her childhood. How could she be? She'd had a wonderful time here with the boys.

But when she'd lost the baby, it felt as if she'd lost everything.

The pasta bubbled fiercely, but the sound of Matt stirring had stopped and she realised he was looking over his shoulder, staring right at her, positively piercing her with his blue eyes.

'You were miles away,' he said. 'What were you thinking? You looked so . . . lost. Do you regret coming back?'

'No,' she said.

He dished up the pasta and placed a plate of hot garlic bread in the middle of the table.

'This looks and smells delicious,' she said. 'I had no idea you were such a good cook.'

'I had a good teacher,' he said and when she gave him a quizzical look, he added, 'Moira.'

He watched her eat, enjoying the sight of her enjoying her food. He had a sudden vision of her, aged about fourteen. She'd changed that year. One moment she'd been a skinny kid with a face full of freckles and the next she'd started showing signs of the woman she was to become. He'd realised, way back then, that his feelings for her might grow into something more than friendship.

'That was really wonderful, Matt,' she said, putting down her fork. He was gratified to see that she'd cleared her plate. 'You'll have to let me cook for you sometime.'

Here they came again, those mixed signals. One minute she was blowing him away, the next she was offering to cook dinner for him. He'd never felt so confused in all his life.

'Tam, I . . . damn!'

The door opened and Denise, one of the receptionists from the surgery annexed to the side of Bay house entered the kitchen.

'Sorry to interrupt your lunch,' she said, then broke off and gave Tam a smile. 'Hi, Tam — good to see you. I've been trying to call you, Matt, then I saw your car outside here. I'm sorry, but you're needed in surgery.'

Matt reached for his jacket and felt in the pocket. He'd left his phone in the car. 'Got to go,' he said apologetically.

* * *

As she stacked the dishwasher, Tam thought if anyone deserved to live their lifelong dream, it was Matt. All he wanted was a wife and children and a proper, stable family home — and she wasn't the person to give it to him.

As she slammed the dishwasher shut, the door opened and Uncle Andrew came in. 'There you are,' he said. 'I want to hear all about your adventures in Australia.'

He held both her hands and looked at her. 'And you can tell me why you're so skinny,' he added. 'Didn't they feed you down under?'

'I'll do a trade,' she said as they entered the house. 'I'll tell you about my adventures if you'll tell me what's been happening to you this past year.'

'Oh, you don't want to hear about that,' he said with a wave of his hand. 'It was nothing. Just a bit of tummy trouble and a bit of a scare with the old ticker. Now your aunt has me on this healthy eating regime, I daren't be ill.'

They went into the lounge which overlooked the back garden and Tam sat down while her uncle poured two coffees.

'I'm supposed to drink decaff,' he said as he handed her a cup. 'But I always reward myself with one cup of the real thing after lunch. So has Matt discussed you shadowing him at all?'

'Shadowing?' Tam looked blank.

'I thought it would be a good idea for you to sit in with him at first so we can ease you back into general practice and you can reacquaint yourself with the way we do things.'

Panic set in. She'd just about convinced herself that she could cope working in the same practice as Matt, bumping into him now and then and having the occasional staff meeting. But shadowing him? Working with him all day every day?

'If I have to shadow someone, can't it be you?'

Andrew laughed. 'Me? I'm a part-timer now, or didn't they tell you? I don't even do house calls any more. No point you shadowing me.'

'What about the other one . . . Adrian, is it?'

'Adrian?' He laughed again. 'Nice enough lad, but he's only a slightly lighter shade of green than you.'

'Thanks,' she said, pleased that her uncle was still teasing her.

'You've no problem working with Matt, have you?' he said, frowning. 'You and he always got along like a house on fire. I even thought for a time there that you might be an item. He was talking about coming out to Australia.' He broke off and his frown deepened. 'I suppose I rather ruined all that for you, didn't I? Damned ulcer. If it hadn't been for me being ill, he would have joined you and who knows what might have happened.'

'There was more to it than that,' Tam protested. 'We just realised we're better off staying friends. It certainly wasn't your fault.'

For the next couple of hours, Tam chatted with her uncle, showing him the photographs she'd brought back with her and giving him the gifts she'd bought him. Then suddenly he looked at his watch and leapt up. 'I'm supposed to be at the gym this afternoon,' he exclaimed. 'Moira will have my guts for garters!'

'The gym?'

'After bullying all my heart attack patients to get down there and get fit, now I find myself in the same boat. You will excuse me, my dear?'

'Of course,' she said warmly. 'Don't overdo it.'

He shook his head at her. 'You're not supposed to say that. You're supposed to tell me to get down there and not even think about coming home until I've worked up a sweat.'

Tam waved him off at the door and no sooner had he gone than Moira's car turned in with Sally in the passenger seat.

'You're looking better already,' Moira said. 'This is Sally. Sally, this is Tamara, my niece. She's the one who . . . '

'I know who she is,' Sally mumbled. 'Thank you for saving my life.'

'I've so much to do,' Moira said. 'Phone calls to make, letters to write. This Sea Festival won't organise itself, and as usual it's been left to me to do everything. I'd much rather sit with you girls and chat, but I can't.'

'We can help,' Tam said. 'Can't we, Sally? I'm sure we could do something useful.'

Moira considered for a moment, then shook her head. 'No, it's all right. I'm going to shut myself in the study and not allow myself to leave until the job is finished.' She hurried away.

'This happens every year,' Tam said. 'She takes it all on and it's far too much work, but she loves every minute of it.'

To her surprise, Sally smiled. 'She's adorable,' she said. 'I was so looking forward to having her as a mother-in-law.'

Tam smiled sympathetically. 'There's no chance of you and Jack . . . ?'

'Not as things stand,' Sally said, her voice becoming bitter. 'He made his feelings perfectly clear before he left.'

'I'm so sorry,' Tam said. 'Jack's always been . . . well, Jack. He can be selfish and thoughtless and when things go wrong, he tends to run away.'

'Tell me about it,' Sally said with a bitter little laugh. 'I'd hardly finished telling him before he was packing his bags and running out of the door.'

'Telling him what?' Tam asked.

'Nothing.' Sally turned away. 'Look if you don't mind, I'll go up to my room. Don't look so worried. I had a long talk with the hospital psychiatrist today and I've promised to be a good girl.'

'If you feel like talking, any time, I'm here. I'll do anything I can to help.'

'It's okay,' Sally said. 'Just because

you saved my life, it doesn't mean you're responsible for my future happiness.'

'I know,' Tam persisted. 'But I also know how it feels when your world falls apart, and I might be able to help. The offer's there if you want it.'

She walked into the living room and was amazed when Sally followed her.

'Actually, you can help,' she said. 'Arrange for me to have a termination.'

The words hung in the air between them. It took Tam a few moments to find her voice.

'How far along are you?'

'About twenty weeks,' Sally answered.

'Twenty weeks,' Tam said softly. 'Have you had any scans? Blood tests, or anything?'

'No point,' Sally said, raising her chin. 'I'm not keeping it. Jack doesn't want it and I certainly don't want to be lumbered with a child I don't want for the next however many years.'

'But what if Jack . . . ?'

'I've given up on Jack,' she said

sharply. 'And I don't want to bring up a child on my own.'

Tam felt a rush of conflicting emotions. She was seeing Sally in a new light. She was a desperate, frightened young woman, not only coping with being cruelly abandoned, but also with rampaging hormones and the prospect of being a mother.

On the other hand, she saw a healthy young woman carrying a presumably healthy baby. By now she would be feeling the first fluttering movements of her child — and yet she wanted to extinguish that life for no better reason than that it would be an inconvenience.

Above all, she felt anger. Anger at her cousin. He should know better. If he was here, now, she'd have a few things to say to him — not least that it was about time he grew up and started behaving responsibly.

'There are other options,' she said hoarsely. 'Besides termination. If you were absolutely sure you didn't want to keep the child . . . '

'I told you, I don't,' Sally snapped.

'You could consider adoption.'

'I've told you what I want to do,' Sally said coldly. 'You're a doctor. You arrange it.'

'I'll be starting work tomorrow,' Tam said softly. She hadn't given up yet on getting Sally to change her mind. 'I'll be working with Matt, but I'll see you on my own at the end of surgery.'

Sally's shoulders slumped. 'Thank you,' she breathed. 'I was kind of hoping you'd understand. Maybe I underestimated you after all.'

She turned and left the room before Tam could say another word. She'd taken her offer to see her at the end of surgery tomorrow as agreement that she'd assist her to end her pregnancy. That hadn't been Tam's intention at all.

If Moira knew that Sally was carrying her grandchild, she'd probably offer to bring it up herself. But Sally wanted closure.

5

Matt saw the last of his patients out and had no sooner closed the door than there was a knock. 'Come in,' he called.

'You're not busy, are you?'

He spun round. 'Tam! I wasn't expecting . . . I mean . . . '

For several months now he'd been erecting a barrier around himself. He'd built it with fast cars and motorbikes and by adopting an almost couldn't-care-less attitude. Yet in a single day she'd got him running round in circles, turning him back into the gibbering idiot she'd reduced him to last year — given to ridiculous fantasies and impossible dreams.

He'd tried to be aloof, uncaring, even abrupt, but he wasn't sure he could keep it up. Maybe he should go for simple professional detachment; treat her as if she were just another young doctor joining the practice for a six-month stint. The trouble was, she wasn't just another young doctor and he was still in love with her.

'Denise said your last patient had just left and I wanted a word with you.'

'Sure, fine,' he said. 'Come in. Close the door. Take a seat. I was just about to sort you out some space for tomorrow.'

There was something different about her. She didn't look so bleak and lost, but now had the look of someone with a purpose about her.

'Is this for me?' she looked at the chair beside his desk.

'Yes, I thought . . . '

Before he could say more, she'd moved it so she was sitting beside him.

'Fine,' he said, fighting the urge to move his own chair away. 'What did you want to see me about?'

'I have a patient who'd like to see me on my own. I was wondering if I could see her after we finish surgery tomorrow?'

'Of course, sure,' he said. 'Why not? Yes.'

'Matt, are you okay?'

'It's been a strange day,' he said, his voice giving away nothing of the turmoil inside him. 'So, tomorrow then. If you'd like to arrange to see your patient at six, I should be finished by then and I can leave you to it.'

'Sounds great.' She smiled — the dazzling smile he remembered her for.

'I'll see you in the morning, then,' he said, hoping she'd take the hint and leave. 'I should get on. Paperwork.'

'Oh, right.' The smile faded as if someone had turned a dimmer switch. It pained him to see the bewilderment on her face. 'I'll leave you to it, then.'

He opened a file on his desk, not looking up because he didn't want to see that spurned-puppy look he knew would be in her eyes.

'Goodnight, then.'

He heard the door close behind her and let out his breath in a rush.

No need to feel guilty. She had it

coming. He laughed a raw laugh. Who was he kidding? There was no satisfaction to be had in giving her the cold shoulder — but there was the small matter of self-preservation. If there was one thing this last year had taught him, it was to look after number one.

* * *

The next morning flew past in a procession of throat infections, strained backs and irritating coughs.

Despite it being the first time they had worked together, they settled into an easy working relationship, acting like a team from the very beginning. Tam was relieved and pleased to find it much easier than she'd imagined.

'Did you know that Jack never wanted to be a doctor?' Matt said when the last morning patient had gone.

She had no idea. She thought Jack was as keen to be a doctor as she and Matt were.

'Obviously not,' Matt said, seeing her

shocked expression. 'I've known for some time, but he hadn't mentioned it for ages. And I thought he'd settled down.'

'But if not a doctor, what on earth did he want to do?'

'That was exactly my reaction. I've never imagined myself doing anything else and I couldn't understand at first why Jack felt the way he did. He wants to be a vet.'

'A vet?' Tam cried. 'And is that what he's going to do now?'

'I have no idea. I haven't heard from him since he left. But I wouldn't be at all surprised if he carves out a whole new life for himself. It's just a pity he couldn't find some space in his new life for Sally.'

'Yes,' Tam murmured.

A knock on the door interrupted them and Denise poked her head round.

'I've a list of house calls for you to make,' she said. 'I'm afraid there are rather a lot.'

'That's fine, Denise,' Matt smiled. 'Are you ready, Tam?'

* * *

Their last house call was to a new mum and her baby.

Tam breathed in the wonderful warm, baby smell that made her heart ache. It was a most peculiar feeling and quite unexpected. It wasn't as if she'd even known that she was pregnant, or had been looking forward to having a baby, when she fell ill — yet just knowing it had existed seemed to haunt her constantly.

Knowing she would never have one of her own haunted her even more.

The young mother looked tired and a little anxious, but one look at the baby told Tam there was nothing to worry about. She was a perfectly beautiful and healthy child.

'I'll let you deal with this, Tam,' Matt said.

'No, it's all right, I . . . '

What was she thinking? Almost every other case today Matt had handed to her to deal with, while he observed. If she was going to start throwing a wobbly every time she came near a baby, he'd suspect something.

'W-would you like to show me the rash?' Tam said shakily. Her palms felt sweaty, her heart was pounding and her mouth was dry. Anxiety symptoms, she knew, but surely she wasn't going to feel like this every time she had to deal with an infant?

The baby was placed on her changing mat and the young mother slipped off the nappy. Tam could see the problem at once.

'Nappy rash,' she said.

'But it looks so red and sore.'

'Yes, it can look very nasty,' Tam said.

'I've been putting lots of talc on to try and keep the area dry, but it's not getting any better.'

'Did you go to parent care classes?' Tam asked, realising at once that she had snapped and regretting it instantly.

She tried to soften her voice. 'Surely you were told there not to use talc?'

'Let's have a look,' Matt interrupted. 'That's a sore little bottom you have there, Chloe.'

Tam made a noise of annoyance and Matt glared at her. The ice in his eyes chilled her to the core. But surely he could see why she was annoyed. Here was a young woman with a beautiful child, causing her all these problems through ignorance. Common sense could have avoided this.

'Best not use talc on the nappy area,' Matt said with a smile.

'You mean this is my fault,' Amanda said and Tam saw that her hand shook as she placed it over her mouth. 'I did this to my baby?'

Now she regretted even more her earlier impatience. What on earth had she been thinking?

'This isn't your fault at all,' she said hastily. 'Babies get nappy rash all the time. That's why there are so many products sold to prevent it. Sometimes it happens for no reason at all, but certain things will exacerbate it once the condition exists.'

'My mum said I never had nappy rash because she used lots of talc,' Amanda explained. 'That's why I ignored the advice. But it just got worse.'

'Sometimes what works for one baby won't work for another,' Tam said.

She gazed down at the baby, who giggled and kicked her legs furiously.

'She loves not wearing a nappy,' she went on. 'Look at her kicking her little legs. Letting the air get to the area is good. Let her have as much time with the nappy off as you can. Oh, you're gorgeous, aren't you?'

Without thinking, Tam leaned forward and picked the baby up, tickling her tummy with the tip of her nose and making her giggle. What a wonderful sound it was — and how empty it made her arms feel when she handed her back to her mother.

'She's a gorgeous baby, Amanda,'

Tam said. 'Very happy. You're obviously doing everything right. If the rash doesn't improve in a day or two, get in touch with us again, but it isn't infected and I'm sure it will clear up quickly now.'

'Thank you,' Amanda said, smiling now, all trace of her anxiety gone.

Matt felt stunned. Stunned at Tam's sharpness, then stunned further by her rapport with the baby. But what had really blown him away was how it felt to see her holding little Chloe. She was a natural, which he thought was probably an extremely chauvinistic thing to think — but for a moment there he'd imagined it was their child she was holding.

And it hit him like a sledgehammer just how much of their future together he'd envisaged before the dream bubble popped.

'I should never have spoken to her like that. I don't know what got into me,' she said now.

'Don't beat yourself up about it,' he

said. 'You realised straight away and made immediate amends.'

He unlocked the car and leaned on it as Tam went round to the other side, looking at her across the roof.

'You were right. She is a gorgeous baby, isn't she?' he said with a grin.

'I didn't really notice. It's just one of those things you say, isn't it?'

She was trying to hide a smile and at the same time avoiding his eyes. He sensed he'd hit some kind of nerve here, but he'd a busy afternoon ahead and there wasn't time to probe deeper into that strange mind of hers now.

'So, who is this patient you're seeing after surgery?' he asked as they got into the car. 'One of Jack's?'

'Not quite,' she said. 'It's Sally.'

'Sally?'

'I can't discuss it with you, Matt,' she cautioned.

'Of course not,' he said. 'But tread carefully. She's . . . '

'Been through a lot. Yes, I know,' Tam sighed.

That was it, he thought. This strange air of tired indifference she could give off. That's what he didn't like and it just didn't match up with the Tam he thought he knew.

'What?' she snapped.

'A little sympathy towards her wouldn't go amiss,' he said.

'What do you think I'm going to do, Matt? Do you honestly think I can't empathise with how she's feeling?'

'Truthfully? I don't think you can, Tam. If you haven't been through it, how can you possibly . . . ?'

'You have no idea what . . . ' she began, her voice shaking as it rose. She turned away from him, but once again he'd caught the pain in her eyes — and she'd very nearly said something. So she *was* hiding something. He knew it. Well, it had taken him long enough, but now the penny had dropped — he could hear it land with a resounding clang.

She'd dumped him for some bronzed, athletic surfer in Australia

— and then the Australian had repaid the favour. So that was it. That was why she'd finally come slinking home. That was why she could look so bleak and haunted at times — because she was thinking of the love she'd lost.

Welcome to the club, he thought harshly.

'I see,' he whispered.

'I don't think you do, Matt,' she answered. 'Hadn't we better get on if we're to go to the hospital and then get back in time to see your afternoon appointments?'

The thought of her being hurt brought no satisfaction.

* * *

Their last patient had been allocated a thirty-minute appointment slot.

'We may be some time with Susanne and her husband,' Matt explained. 'She's been through a lot over the past few years.'

But when the woman walked through

the door, she was alone. The strain of what she'd been going through showed in every line on her pale face.

Before she could speak, Matt said softly, 'I know, Susanne. I have the paperwork here. I'm so sorry.'

Then he turned to Tam.

'Susanne has just had her eighth attempt at conceiving by IVF. Sadly it was unsuccessful.'

Suddenly the floodgates opened. Susanne leaned forward in her chair and grasped Matt's hand, her desperation evident.

'You have to ask them to try one more time. We can't afford any more private treatments. Gary refuses to borrow another penny to fund it. He says we're just throwing good money after bad. But we can't give up now! We've been so close.'

When Matt spoke, his voice was gentle.

'If I could, I would, you know that, but our health authority is strict on this. Under their current guidelines they will only offer one attempt.'

'It's not my fault that I can't conceive,' Susanne burst out. 'I have endometriosis and I've tried everything. IVF was our last hope.'

Tam could only imagine what Susanne had been through, the raising of hopes and the bitter disappointment every time yet another treatment failed.

'Why didn't Gary come with you today, Susanne?' Matt asked.

'Refused,' she said, lowering her head. 'He said no more. But my marriage is over if this is the end, Matt. And I'm not getting any younger.'

Life and circumstances had broken this woman's spirit and, quite possibly, her marriage.

'He'll find someone else,' she said desperately. 'I know he will. Someone who can give him children. You've seen him, Matt. You know how much he wants kids.'

'Susanne . . . '

'No,' she cried. 'You have no idea what it's like for me to repeatedly disappoint him, to see the hurt look on his face every time I have to tell him that I've failed yet again.'

'*You* haven't failed, Susanne,' Matt said. 'The treatment has failed.'

'How can you possibly understand?' Susanne cried. 'You wouldn't have to think twice if you wanted a child. You'd just take it for granted that it would happen, just as Gary and I did at first.'

She drew in her breath. Her eyes clouded with more tears.

'I just don't know what more I can possibly do,' Susanne cried out.

Matt glanced at Tam. She got to her feet and placed her hand on Susanne's arm, longing to tell her that she knew how she felt. She had that void inside her too, but it was something she had to keep to herself.

To her surprise, Susanne turned and sobbed against her shoulder. Tam held her while Matt looked on, his eyes brooding and dark, his expression impossible to read.

At last Susanne pulled away and

groped for the tissue Tam had ready for her. 'Sorry,' she whispered. 'I just don't . . . I can't stand any more.'

'You have every right to be upset,' Tam said gently.

'I just feel that no one understands,' Susanne sobbed. 'Not even Gary.'

The one person who had been through all this with her — and she no longer felt she could even turn to him. Tam found that the most heartbreaking thing of all. They had been through all this as a couple, and now Susanne was on her own.

She looked at Matt through a blur of her own tears and tried to blink them away, but one trickled down her cheek. Matt saw and frowned slightly.

'Maybe a cup of tea . . . ' he said. Tam, relieved, immediately left the room.

By the time she got back to the surgery with the tea, Susanne had gone and Matt was tapping away at his computer keyboard. He looked up.

'She left shortly after you,' he said.

'For what it's worth, I think that hug you gave her helped a lot. She feels very much on her own, but I think her husband is right and it's time to call it a day.'

Tam's hand shook as she placed the cup on his desk. Did he really mean what she thought he meant — that Gary Bond should find himself a younger, more fertile wife?

'Oh, I'm sorry,' he said. 'It's almost six. Sally will be here any minute. I'll get out of your way and leave you to it. You may as well drink the tea.'

'But what about Susanne?' she asked. 'Isn't there anything more that can be done?'

'Only if she can find the money to fund more treatment.' He shrugged. 'Which is apparently out of the question. It's a shame, but there you are.'

'I can't believe you're being so cold about this, Matt.'

'Cold? No. Realistic maybe. It's time for them to move on.'

'What if it was you, Matt? What if you were married, and your wife couldn't give you children?'

He stared at her for a moment. 'I'm not married,' he said. 'Nor am I likely to be. So it's not a question I have to answer.'

He picked up some folders and breezed out of the room. Tam sank into his just vacated chair and sighed. *Time to move on*. If only it were that easy.

6

'This isn't easy for me you know,' Sally said, hesitating by the open door. 'I almost didn't come.'

'I know. It must be very difficult,' Tam said. 'Please, come in. We won't be disturbed.'

After a moment of indecision, Sally closed the door and sat down.

'You're going to help me sort this out, aren't you?'

'That's why we're here,' Tam said. 'I take it you've done a test?'

'Three,' Sally mustered a rueful smile. 'The result of the first test delighted me. Then I spoke to Jack and did another test and this time, I prayed it would be negative. Same with the third.'

Tam's eyebrows rose slightly.

'You were delighted? You wanted the baby?'

'Of course I did. I love Jack. I thought the baby would cement our relationship. The thought of carrying his child . . . ' She smiled softly and for the first time, Tam glimpsed the real Sally. 'Well, it filled me with joy, Tam.'

'That much hasn't changed, you know,' Tam said. 'You're still carrying his child. It's the same baby inside you, whatever is happening externally.'

'I know that.' Sally squeezed her eyes tight shut as if trying to fight back tears. 'But I can't cope with a child on my own.'

'A lot of people do,' Tam pointed out.

'I'm not a lot of people,' Sally sighed. 'I'm me. And if I get rid of the baby, maybe Jack . . . '

'I see,' Tam said, leaning back in her chair. 'But what if you get rid of the baby and Jack doesn't come back?'

Sally got to her feet. 'I don't know,' she cried. 'I'm so confused — and scared. Why didn't you just leave me to die, Tam? If you hadn't interfered, this would all be over for me now. You ruined everything.'

She began to sob, not just the tears of someone deeply upset, but gut wrenching howls that tore at Tam's heart. Tam was out of her chair and round the desk in a moment, her arms reaching around Sally.

'Oh, love,' she said. 'He's not worth it. No man is worth all this.'

'But I love him,' Sally groaned. 'It's an ache deep inside me, a gnawing pain that just won't go away. And now there's this child and I just don't know what to do.'

Tam led her back to her chair and sat her down.

'You really are confused aren't you, love?' she said. 'I don't think you're in any state to make a decision on a termination. You can't do something as life-changing as that without it having repercussions, and I'm afraid if you go ahead with it, then you're just going to feel worse in the long run.'

Sally stopped crying. Her face was red and tear-streaked and she looked for a long time at Tam.

'You talk as if you've had personal experience,' she said at last.

Tam straightened up and made no comment, but turned instead to Matt's wall calendar. Personal experience, yes — of losing a child. Different, maybe, but in time Sally would feel that loss too, and it could destroy her. Tam wouldn't wish that kind of pain on anyone.

'Let's do some blood tests and book you in for a scan.'

'What's the point?' Sally said dully.

'Well, we need to confirm your dates before we do anything else,' Tam pointed out.

It struck her as so ironic that the last patient she'd seen was desperate to have a child while Sally wasn't even sure if she wanted to keep hers. How cruel nature could be sometimes.

'I'll arrange it all first thing tomorrow, and let you know what time to be at the hospital. I'll come with you if you like.'

'Would you? I'd like that.'

Tam went back to her seat and filled out a form. 'Take this with you, and get your blood test done while you're at the hospital.'

'Thanks,' Sally said, mustering a weak watery smile.

They left the surgery together. Outside, Tam stopped.

'I'm going for a short walk,' she said. 'Will you tell my aunt I'll be home in about fifteen minutes?'

'Of course,' Sally said, then she added. 'Thank you, Tam.'

'What for?'

'Understanding about me wanting a termination,' she said. 'It's almost as if you've been through it yourself. I feel that you know how I feel — does that make sense to you?'

Tam squeezed her arm. 'Yes, it does. Like I said, I'll come to the hospital with you tomorrow and we'll take it from there. Right now you should go and get in the warm,' she said. 'I'll be home shortly.'

She watched as Sally made her way to the front of the house and waited until the front door had closed behind her before turning to begin her walk.

As she turned, she walked straight into something solid.

'Matt!' she gasped. 'What on earth are you doing here, lurking about in the darkness?'

'I work here, remember?' he said coldly. 'And I wasn't lurking. I'm about to go on a home visit and I was coming back to the surgery to pick up one or two things.'

It was hard to read his expression in the darkness, but his eyes were glittering and there was something about his demeanour that alarmed her.

'Matt, what's wrong?'

'Wrong?' He was breathing hard, almost as if he was struggling to keep himself under control. 'What could possibly be wrong? I'll see you in the morning at eight.'

He swung away from her, marching

towards the surgery, each angry footstep crunching on the gravel. Tam shivered. Had he overheard her conversation with Sally? Well — if he had, what could he have made of it?

She tried to recall what had been said, but couldn't as she walked slowly to the end of the drive and looked down along the coastal path. Perhaps she'd leave the walk for another time. She shivered, her skin suddenly feeling chilled.

It was a clear night, the moon was high and bright and casting diamond lights on the sea. The glittering lights reminded her of Matt's eyes. Not sparkling with happiness or affection, but with something closer to hatred.

But why? Things had seemed to be settling down. They'd had a good day working together.

She heard a roar behind her and jumped to one side as Matt came out of the drive on the Ducati. She watched as he sped down the coast road, his red tail light disappearing rapidly into the distance.

'Oh, Matt,' she whispered. 'What have I done wrong now?'

* * *

Matt ground his teeth. She had some nerve, accusing him of being cold when he'd just heard her discussing a termination with Sally as if they were planning some kind of cosy shopping trip.

It had come as a double shock to him. The first being Sally's pregnancy, the second being Tam's apparent willingness — eagerness, almost — to assist her in getting a termination. And what was that about Tam knowing how Sally felt? How on earth could she, unless . . .

He pushed thoughts of Tam to the back of his mind. The next few hours were going to be tough enough without making it worse.

* * *

The next morning as Tam walked into reception, she heard Matt's voice over the intercom system and it wasn't the relaxed, friendly voice of yesterday. Today his voice was laced with impatience.

'Has Dr Lawrence arrived yet, Denise?'

Denise looked up and smiled. 'Just walked in, Matt,' she said.

'I'm not late,' Tam said, checking her watch against the clock on the wall as she hurried towards the corridor leading to Matt's room. Ridiculous to feel so nervous, yet she felt almost like a tardy latecomer on her first day.

Matt burst through the door as she approached, almost colliding with her in the corridor.

'I'm not late,' she repeated.

'I know, I'm just glad you're here,' he said, although he looked anything but pleased to see her. 'Would you see my appointments this morning?'

He pushed his hand through his already untidy hair and when he looked at her, his eyes seemed bleached of colour. Probably an effect of the dark shadow of stubble on his face, Tam thought, which in itself was strange. Matt wasn't the sort to turn up for work unshaven with uncombed hair. But then, he hadn't been the sort to ride a motorbike like some sort of demon out of hell either.

She watched him go and noticed the collar of his shirt was sticking up on one side, poking above the collar of his jacket and she itched to chase after him and straighten it. But before he reached the end of the corridor, he'd straightened it himself.

Before turning into the reception area, he squared his shoulders and straightened up. Brave face for the world. *But why, Matt, why?*

She shivered. The way he was behaving reminded her of Jack. A couple of years ago, before Matt joined the practice, she'd been here for a long weekend and Jack had turned up for work looking like that. He was obviously hung over and hadn't even bothered to change his shirt, which was crumpled and had lipstick stains all over it.

Andrew had been furious and had given his son a dressing-down on the spot, sending him home to clean up his act.

What was Matt trying to do here? Turn himself into a clone of her cousin? If he was, then it wouldn't work — because Matt didn't possess that selfish streak no matter how hard he tried to pretend he did.

She turned and headed for his room when another door opened and Adrian smiled out at her.

'Matt told you about the change this morning? If you're having any problems, just give me a buzz. And if you feel that you can't manage the home visits — '

'I'll manage,' Tam said lightly. 'Matt's obviously got something more important to deal with. What is it? Woman trouble?'

Adrian was already on his way back into his room, but stopped and turned to look at her.

'Woman trouble? Matt?' He laughed incredulously. 'You have to be kidding. That guy doesn't have time to have woman trouble. In all honesty, I wish he did, because the way he's been acting lately, he'll grind himself into the ground.'

'So what's going on?'

'He didn't tell you? He's with a patient. Sad case. Young man.' He shook his head. 'He wants to die at home, family around him. He's hanging on by a thread. The family are just about holding it together — you know how it is.'

'Yes,' Tam whispered.

'You know Matt,' Adrian said. 'He said he'd be there for the family when the time came and he'll stand by that. For the past few weeks, all we've been able to offer the patient is palliative care.'

She stepped into Matt's office and

closed the door behind her. No wonder he'd been so tense last night — and again this morning. He must be exhausted as well as emotionally drained.

She seated herself at Matt's desk and looked quickly through her list for the morning.

'Everything okay?' Uncle Andrew asked, popping his head in.

'Everything is fine,' Tam smiled. And it was, too. She felt ready for this. More than ready. 'I'm just about to call my first patient.'

'Good,' he beamed. 'Can I have a word later when you've a moment?'

'Sounds serious.'

'Not really. I just want to ask a favour. I'd like to speak to Matt too, but I'm not sure today would be the best time. See you later.'

* * *

There was such a sense of relief in the room. Matt could feel it, almost as a tangible presence. The feeling of *Thank God it's all over* and the realisation that the very last hope had gone. For although the family were fully aware that there would be no miracle recovery for Gavin and wanted him to be free of his pain, it was human nature to cling to that last tiny shred of hope, however impossible it seemed.

'I'll be in the other room,' he said softly.

'No, please stay,' Gavin's mother said, looking at her family for confirmation.

'You've been as much a part of this as we have,' her husband said, holding on to Matt's arm. 'Please, stay with us for a while.'

Matt nodded, biting hard into his lip. The young man was at peace now, and perhaps his family could finally find some peace too. They'd been through a terrible ordeal which had seemed to go on forever, but now it was over it was as if it had happened in the blink of an eye.

After a while he put his hand on Gavin's mother's shoulder and gave it a light squeeze.

'I'm going to go and make some tea,' he said.

'Thank you,' she whispered, covering his hand with her own and squeezing back. 'For everything, Matt.'

* * *

This was how Tam liked her life to be. Busy. The hours passing by in a blur. And now, in her lunch break, she was sitting in the maternity unit at the hospital with Sally.

Until they stepped through the door, she hadn't thought about her own feelings or how she would react to being here. But however she felt, she knew it was something she would have to face and overcome as so many women did.

'Why did I have to come here?' Sally asked.

'It's where they do the scans, that's

all,' Tam explained. 'Don't worry. I'm not going to start parading babies in front of you in the hope of making you change your mind.'

Sally smiled ruefully. 'I know, I'm sorry. It's just making me nervous, all this. I can hear a baby crying, too.'

And it's probably tearing you apart just the same as it is me, Tam thought.

'That's why I'm here,' she said, her voice giving nothing away of the turmoil inside. 'To hold your hand.'

'Here goes,' Tam said when Sally's name was called. 'Come on. It'll be all right. Do you want me to come in with you?'

'Definitely,' Sally said. 'I can't do this on my own.'

While the scan was done and measurements were taken, Sally kept casting nervous glances at Tam. She smiled back and squeezed her hand, but it was hard not to stare at the images on the screen.

'That all seems fine, your measurements certainly back up your dates and the baby looks perfect,' Judith said cheerfully. 'I'll see if I can get a good picture of baby for you now.'

Tam wasn't sure who looked the most eagerly at the screen, her or Sally, as Judith moved the scanner over Sally's small bump.

'She's an active little thing,' Judith chuckled.

'She?' Sally whispered.

'I don't like calling them 'it',' Judith explained. 'And I can't tell what sex the baby is. Even if I could, it's Trust policy not to tell parents. Are you hoping for a boy or a girl?'

Sally replied immediately, 'I don't mind, as long as it's . . . '

She broke off and bit her lip.

'Here we go,' Judith said triumphantly. 'There she is.'

As soon as she saw the fuzzy blur that was her baby, Sally began to cry. But they were tears of joy. Tam had taken a gamble and it had paid off. If Sally had gone ahead with a termination, she would have suffered later.

Maybe not for a year, maybe not for ten years, but eventually she would. She'd wanted this baby at first and that hadn't changed. She still wanted it.

'You're crying too,' Sally remarked.

'Am I?' Tam laughed. 'Well, it's a beautiful sight, isn't it?'

To her utter amazement, Sally hugged her. 'Thank you, Tam,' she said.

Tam held her tight. *This could have been me*, she thought. *If not for a hideous mistake made by nature, I would have carried my own child*. She felt dangerously close to losing it and had to bite down hard on her lip.

'Are you all right?' Judith looked with concern at Tam as she straightened up. 'Your lip is bleeding.'

'Is it?' Tam laughed it off and wiped away the blood with her finger. 'Oh, it's nothing.'

7

'I'm sorry I left you without warning,' Matt said as he breezed into his office late in the afternoon. 'Any problems?'

How different he looked now to how he had this morning. He was clean-shaven, his hair was tidy and still damp from the shower and apart from the dark circles under his eyes, there was no sign of his weariness.

'Nothing I couldn't handle,' she said. 'Are you all right?'

'Of course. Why shouldn't I be?'

'Denise told me that Gavin died today,' she said. 'I'm sorry.'

'I'm not,' he said, rather too harshly. 'He'd been suffering for too long. It was what Moira would call a happy release. Any messages for me? Anything I need to know?'

Clearly, he didn't want to discuss the matter.

'Yes, there is something,' she said. 'Andrew and Moira would like you to join us for dinner this evening. But they'd quite understand if you wanted to have an early night.'

He stopped rifling through patient notes and looked up at her.

'Would you prefer me to turn down the invitation?'

'Of course not,' she said. 'Whatever gives you that idea?'

'All right. I'll be there. I've a few letters to write and some other matters to attend to. I'll be round in plenty of time for dinner.'

She got up from the chair and he sat straight down in it, immediately taking a patient's notes from their envelope.

'Matt,' Tam said softly. 'If there's anything I can do . . . '

He looked up at her, fixed her with that penetrating blue gaze and without any kind of emotion said, 'I think you've done enough, don't you?'

Now what on earth did that mean?

He's tired, she reminded herself. He

was up all night and hadn't had time to catch any rest during the day. No wonder he wasn't making much sense. She realised he was still looking at her, his lips pressed together, waiting for her to leave.

She closed the surgery door quietly behind her and headed for home.

* * *

'That was a delicious meal, Moira,' Matt said as Moira brought coffee to the table. 'Thank you for inviting me over.'

'I'll clear some of these things away,' Tam said and started to stack the dishes. Sally immediately began to help.

Incredibly, or perhaps not, Matt had cleared his plate. He probably hadn't eaten for over twenty-four hours and now that he had had a good meal, his eyes had taken on a heavy tiredness that made Tam's heart ache for him.

'Leave the dishes for the moment,' Andrew said. 'We had an ulterior motive for asking you over tonight, Matt. There's something we'd like to discuss with you and Tam.'

'I'll go,' Sally said, starting to rise to her feet.

'Of course you won't,' Moira said. 'Sit down, dear. We just want to talk about the Sea Festival, that's all.'

'Ah,' Matt said. 'That's all, is it?'

Andrew laughed. 'He knows what's coming, Moira,' he said. 'He knows he's about to be roped in whether he likes it or not.'

'Well, thank you for jumping in with both feet as usual,' Moira said. 'I was going to lead up to asking them and now you've probably put them off.'

'Ask us what, Aunt Moira?' Tam said. 'Are you going to let us help after all?'

'It's the novelty raft race,' Moira said. 'I'd like you to organise it for me. It's a matter of getting in the entries and on the day, checking that they comply with the rules.'

'That should be easy,' Matt said. 'What rules?'

Moira smiled sheepishly. 'That's the other thing. I'd like you to draw up a list of rules. Just with a mind to safety.'

'If the two of you get your heads together over this, I'm sure you can come up with something,' Andrew said. 'There, Moira. I told you they wouldn't mind.'

Mind? Tam couldn't think of anything worse at the moment than getting her head anywhere near Matt's.

'I'm sure it doesn't need two of us,' she said.

She looked across the table at Matt. In the dusky light cast by the flickering candles on the table, his face was wreathed in inky shadows.

'Tam's right,' he murmured. 'I'll do it on my own.'

'Nonsense,' Andrew said. 'You're both hard pushed. With you working together, the workload will be halved. And besides, it should be fun.'

Tam flinched under Matt's heavy, hooded gaze and wondered if anyone else in the room had noticed — and if they had, what did they make of it?

'When do you want us to start?' he asked.

'As soon as possible,' Moira said. 'We could have a meeting about it at the weekend. You could come for lunch, Matt. Sunday? Will you still be here, Sally?'

Sally took a deep breath. 'Actually, Moira,' she said. 'I was going to ask you if I could stay on here indefinitely. I'm going to look for a job in the area at least . . . temporarily. And then later . . . oh, I'm jumping the gun.'

Moira, who was always on the ball and could usually sense what was coming, suddenly sat upright. On her face was an expression of anticipation, almost excitement.

'Yes, dear?'

'I'm pregnant,' Sally said on an outward rush of breath. 'I'm expecting Jack's baby.'

'Oh my Lord!' Moira gasped, then she was on her feet, rushing round the table and hugging Sally. 'This is wonderful news.'

Tam looked back at Matt and he was still staring at her, not at Sally, as if Tam's reaction was more important to him than anyone else's.

'Congratulations,' Andrew said, his voice slightly shaky with surprise. 'So I'm to be a grandfather! Does Jack . . . I mean, is he aware . . . '

'Yes,' Sally said. 'He knows. But I've been doing a lot of thinking. I want this baby, whether Jack is interested or not. I had a scan today . . . '

She got up from the table and fetched her bag.

'I have a scan picture. Would anyone like to see?'

'Would we?' Moira cried.

Sally pulled the picture out of her bag and handed it to Moira.

'Meet your grandchild, Moira.'

'Oh, how lovely,' Moira whispered. 'Oh, Sally, I can't tell you . . . '

She stopped and looked at Tam, almost as if she felt guilty for allowing herself to feel such joy. The pain on her face was so raw that Tam spoke quickly to reassure her.

'It's wonderful news, isn't it?' she said.

'You knew about all this? How?' Moira demanded, her brow creasing.

'Tam took me for a scan at lunchtime,' Sally said.

There was a harsh sound as Matt's chair scraped back from the table.

'It's marvellous news, Sally,' he said, stooping to kiss her. 'I'm delighted for you. I'd love to stay and celebrate the news with you too, but I'm bushed. I'm not very good company tonight.'

He turned then to kiss Moira.

'Thanks for a lovely meal,' he said. 'I don't think I would have bothered cooking anything for myself.'

'Of course you wouldn't,' Moira said, reaching up to push his hair away from his face. 'It's been a rotten day for you. You get home and off to bed and get some rest. We'll talk about the festival at the weekend when you're feeling a bit more with it.'

'And I'm so happy for you,' he added. 'And pleased for the baby. She'll have terrific grandparents — the best.'

'Thank you,' Moira said.

'Goodnight, Andrew,' he said, then nodding towards Tam added shortly, 'Tam.'

'I'll see you out,' Tam said, getting up from the table.

Moira and Andrew were asking Sally questions and already discussing which room would be the baby's.

'I can find my own way out,' Matt said as she followed him into the hall.

'What have I done, Matt?' she asked. 'Why are you so angry with me?'

'I'm not angry with you,' he muttered. 'I'm just tired.'

She should have left it there, accepted that as his reason. But he'd been friendly towards everyone else.

'I don't buy that,' she said flatly.

They'd reached the front door.

'Why don't you quit while you're ahead, Tam?' he asked wearily.

'You sound so bitter. Aren't you

pleased about the baby?'

'I'm delighted for them,' he said, then sighed heavily. 'Angry with Jack, I guess — and still trying to figure you out. Last night I overheard you discussing a termination with Sally. You must be feeling pretty disappointed that she's gone against your wishes.'

Tam's heart slammed against her ribs. He surely didn't mean what she thought he meant. That she might actively encourage anyone to end a perfectly healthy pregnancy?

'My *wishes*?'

'Goodnight, Tam.'

And before she could say a word in her own defence, he'd gone, striding off down the path to be swallowed by the darkness.

* * *

'Fool,' Matt muttered furiously as he turned into the gates of his cottage. 'Damn fool.'

But he'd got it figured out now

— got her figured out. It all fell neatly in to place, the whole rotten scenario. There wasn't another guy involved; he had been wrong with that assumption. But there *had* been someone else; a little tiny someone without a voice.

That night, her last night, he hadn't taken precautions — hadn't even asked her if she was taking the contraceptive pill.

And then once she was in Australia there had been the long, loving phone calls. The promises. The plans for the future. Everything had been great — and then suddenly, overnight, it all changed.

About two months after she left England, in fact. Around the time she'd have been confirming a pregnancy. And presumably Moira was in on the whole thing. That would be why she hadn't told Tam about Andrew's illness.

That was her 'urgent business at the hospital' that had stopped her speaking to him on the phone. It wasn't work at all.

He thrust his key into the lock and twisted it, shoving the door open, then slamming it hard behind him. He squeezed his eyes tight shut and his heart ached for the child that wouldn't be.

Well you wanted to know why she dumped you, he thought. *Now you do*. But he wished to God he didn't.

* * *

'We've already had six entries for the raft race,' Matt said as Tam joined him in Moira's study after lunch on Sunday.

'That's great news,' Tam said. 'All we have to do now is sort out some rules and find a time slot in the day.'

'I've got the tide tables here,' Matt said. 'High tide will be at three-thirty, so if we hold the race at one, we'll have plenty of water in the harbour to float the boats, but it should be all finished before the tide turns. I don't want to risk any of the entrants being washed out to sea.'

‘Good thinking,’ Tam agreed.

He made a few notes, then turned his pad to show Tam and for a brief moment, his eyes met hers before he averted them. It had been like this all week, with Matt struggling to keep up a professionally detached front.

‘Looks good to me,’ she said. ‘You’re the lifeboat man, so you’ll know what you’re doing as regards safety.’

‘Fine. As long as we agree, I think we’re probably done,’ he said. ‘But Moira will never believe we’ve got it sorted in ten minutes.’

Tam laughed. ‘You know what she’s like. If we come out and say we’ve finished, she’ll send us back in here and tell us to do it properly and not show our faces until we have.’

Matt looked over at the window. ‘Of course, we needn’t stay in here,’ he said. ‘It’s a lovely day. Do you fancy a walk? I could do with some air.’

He strode across to the window and pushed it open.

‘Well are you coming?’ he said,

holding out his hand ready to help her over the low ledge into the garden.

'I don't know, Matt,' she whispered.

'You wouldn't have hesitated twenty years ago,' he said. 'In fact, I remember you doing exactly that.'

'You remember that?' Tam cried.

'Of course I do. We'd all been sent in here to await a ticking-off for something you'd done, and you and Jack decided to leg it. So when Moira came in, I was the only one left, waiting patiently for my punishment.'

Tam rested her hand in his and leaned on him as she climbed out of the window. The air was cool, but the promise of summer was in the air, Tam could feel it. He didn't release her hand once she was standing outside beside him.

'That was mean of us,' she said. 'Leaving you behind.'

He looked down at her. 'Story of my life,' he said. 'You and Jack, always taking off somewhere, leaving me to clear up behind you.'

He squeezed her hand lightly, almost regretfully, then let go of it and walked away.

'You coming?' he called over his shoulder.

She had to run to keep up with him. Her leg was feeling much better now and apart from the odd twinge, wasn't giving her any trouble.

Matt reached the safety rail at the top of the cliff ages before she did and when he got there, he turned to face her, watching her approach, the expression in his eyes unreadable.

She stood beside him, leaning on the rail facing out to sea.

'I've been thinking,' he said. 'About Sally's baby.'

Tam held her breath.

'It's going to be tough raising a child alone, even with Moira and Andrew's support. Sally's not a strong person, as you've probably realised. I think that's what may have scared Jack off. She might have come across as a bit needy.'

'It's no excuse,' Tam said crossly. She

still felt angry with Jack and probably always would.

'I'm the last person to make excuses for him,' Matt said. 'But he's my best friend. He always has been. He's a good man deep down and what I plan to do is as much for him as for Sally and the baby.'

Tam pushed back from the rail and looked at him.

'What are you saying, Matt?'

'The baby needs a father, that's all,' he said. 'And I intend to see she gets just that.'

The words hung in the air between them, but to Tam they said everything. He'd never loved her — not in the way she'd loved him. He'd loved the idea of marriage, children and the stability of a family. He could have all that with Sally. *And let's not forget*, Tam thought bitterly, *she's beautiful as well as pregnant*.

'I think you're right,' she said at last.

This was what she wanted, wasn't it? Matt settled and happy? But was it realistic to even imagine she could stick around under such circumstances?

'Good,' he said. 'But don't mention it to Sally just yet.'

'Don't worry, I won't.'

She turned and hurried back towards the house.

8

Matt caught up with her just before she turned into the gates of Bay House. It wasn't difficult. She tired easily and she'd started to limp.

He reached out, grabbed her arm and turned her to face him, then stepped back shocked to see her face wet with tears. Not just wet — soaked. Her eyes looked huge and full of sorrow and her lips trembled in a way that tore lumps out of his heart.

'Tam — what on earth?'

She couldn't speak and tried to turn her face away, obviously not wanting him to see her like this. He wrapped his arms around her and pulled her close. She struggled weakly at first, then relaxed against him, sobbing silently against his chest.

Her head was just beneath his chin and it didn't take much to kiss her hair.

He hated what she'd done to him, but he couldn't bring himself to hate her. He'd tried. And there was still that niggling doubt worrying away at the back of his mind that he was wrong, so wrong about her.

And it tore him apart seeing her like this. Seeing her so unhappy. Tam had always been such a bright, happy kid and the Tam he'd fallen in love with last year had been just as in love with life, with living. But this little lass in his arms was a tiny, trembling, fearful child and he knew that in some way he was responsible for her unhappiness.

'Tam, love,' he said raggedly. 'We need to talk.'

'No,' she pleaded. 'There's nothing to say.'

He moved forward to kiss her and somehow she didn't move away. When their lips touched, hers were full and trembling, like a bird fluttering against his mouth.

'Tell me you don't love me,' he demanded.

'I can't,' she cried. 'Don't do this to me, Matt.'

'Why not? We have to talk, Tam. Just look at what this is doing to us.'

She pushed back from him, ran the back of her hands fiercely across her cheeks to wipe away the tears.

'There's nothing to say,' she repeated brokenly.

'I think we have plenty to say to each other, don't you? You have to tell me what it is, Tam. If we're going to have any kind of relationship, then I have to know what has hurt you so much.'

'Relationship?'

She looked up at him. Her eyes had darkened with the tears and he saw such trust reflected there that he knew there was no going back until he found out what was at the root of her unhappiness. He held the key to her future just as much as she held the key to his.

But he couldn't go charging in like a mad bull.

'Look, I want to get Sally sorted out.

The sooner I can get Jack back here to face up to his responsibilities . . . '

'Jack?' Her eyes widened.

'I know where he is, Tam. He's in Thailand — he called me a couple of days ago. If you and Adrian are willing to hold the fort, I plan to go out there and talk to him. But not a word to Sally. I don't want to raise her hopes.'

Tam rubbed again at her selfish, stupid tears. Why had she been upset? Because for one moment she thought that Matt might have found happiness with someone else and she couldn't bear it? It would happen eventually and she'd have to get used to the idea.

Right now, though, he was gazing down at her as if she meant all the world to him.

'Don't get me wrong,' he said. 'I'm not going to force the guy to marry someone he doesn't love — but you should have seen those two together, Tam. It was like watching a storm — dramatic and exciting. I think he wants to come home, but doesn't know how. Do you know what I mean?'

His question was concerned with more than Jack's feelings. He was giving Tam the opportunity to tell him about the past year, but she couldn't.

She'd thought about it often enough. If she told him about the baby they'd lost, then he'd feel sorry for her and sooner or later he'd grow to resent her and she couldn't bear that.

'I love you, Tam,' he said.

'No, you don't,' she said resolutely. 'You can't. We'd better get back inside before we're missed.'

She turned to walk away, but he caught her arm and swung her round to face him again.

'Why can't I? What happened to you last year, Tam?'

Tam mustered all her resolve. There weren't going to be any more tears.

'This isn't the time or the place,' she said levelly, despite the fact that her body was reacting to the touch of his hand on her arm. Gentle but firm, his fingers pressing lightly, bringing back sweet but painful memories. She closed her eyes so that she didn't have to look at him.

'When I get back from Thailand,' he murmured. 'We'll talk then, Tam. And we'll talk properly.'

'When will you go?'

'It's Gavin's funeral on Tuesday,' he said with a sigh. 'I'll go as soon as I can after that.'

* * *

Coming to a decision had made a big difference to Sally. She was positively glowing.

'It was a bit sudden, wasn't it, this family crisis Matt had to rush away for?' she remarked as Tam flew round the kitchen snatching a bite to eat before rushing back to work.

'I suppose it was,' Tam said. 'But these things happen.'

'I bet you miss him.'

'It won't be for long,' she said,

smiling. 'He's only been gone for a week and Adrian and I are coping.'

'No, I mean you miss him, personally.'

'Absolutely not,' Tam said.

'Come on,' Sally laughed. 'Anyone can see you're in love with him. And Jack said you two were practically engaged when you went to Australia.'

'Well Jack was wrong,' Tam said briskly, reaching for her bag. 'Matt and I are just . . . '

'Good friends,' Sally finished for her. 'And I'm the Queen of Sheba. Hey, Tam, you haven't seen my scan picture around anywhere, have you? I can't find it anywhere.'

Tam smiled, relieved that the subject had been changed. 'Aunt Moira's probably taken it to show all her friends. You know how excited she is about the baby.'

'Ah,' Sally laughed. 'That will be it.'

* * *

Tam glanced up at the sky as she got out of the car back at Bay House after doing her rounds. Storm clouds were gathering over the sea and the wind was picking up.

As she opened the door to her room, she was already shrugging off her jacket and nearly jumped out of her skin when someone helped her off with it and familiar fingers brushed her neck, setting her skin on fire.

'You're back!' she cried before she could stop herself. She hadn't meant to sound quite so delighted and for two pins, if common sense hadn't prevailed, she'd have thrown her arms around Matt and hugged him.

Matt hung her jacket on the peg, then turned to face her. She hadn't seen him look this happy since — well since before she went away.

'Mission accomplished,' he announced with satisfaction. 'Jack's at the house now, talking to Sally.'

'Oh, that's brilliant! Was it difficult persuading him to come home?'

'Not when I pointed out that most men would kill for what he had waiting for him at home. A woman he loves, a child on the way and parents willing to support him while he trains to be a vet.'

He smiled and reached into his pocket.

'I took this with me,' he said, showing Tam Sally's scan picture. 'I forgot to give it back to her just now, but once she saw Jack, I think the picture was the last thing on her mind. Once Jack saw his baby, the rest was easy. And now that I'm back again, you and I can have that talk, can't we?'

Tam ran her tongue across her lips. Talking to Matt was the last thing she wanted to do.

'I've got patients waiting.'

'I've waited a year,' he said. 'A few more hours won't make any difference.'

He grazed her cheek with the back of his hand.

'I love you, Tam. That much hasn't changed. I had a lot of time to think sitting on the plane and I realised life's too short to waste any of it whatever might have happened in the past.'

She leaned her head into his hand and closed her eyes and cursed herself for not being stronger.

Straightening up, she reached for his hand and pushed it away.

'There is nothing for us to talk about,' she said coldly. 'We spent one night together, that's all. You don't even know me so don't imagine you're in love with me. I don't love you, Matt.'

'That's what you say,' he said and before she could react, he kissed her, not gently like before, but fiercely, possessively and despite all her good intentions, she responded hungrily.

This time it was he who pushed her away and held her at arm's length. His eyes burned with desire.

'You don't love me or you do? Which is it?' he growled.

'I don't,' she gasped, now that he was far enough away for her to drag herself kicking and screaming back to her senses. 'I don't love you. I never loved you and I will never love you. Do you understand? There is no future for us.'

Matt flinched, then tightened his lips.

'Message received,' he said. 'Loud and clear.'

Then he turned on his heel and walked out.

Tam stumbled to her desk and leaned on it, breathing hard. This should have been easy — and would have been, if only Matt had played by the rules.

Denise buzzed through a few minutes later and asked if she could see Susanne and Gary Bond.

'Of course,' Tam said. 'Send them down.'

The moments as she waited for them to arrive felt like the longest of her life. Were they going to plead for another try at IVF? Would it be fair of her to encourage them to try again?

What a pleasant surprise it was when the couple walked in. Susanne looked much happier and the lines of strain were gone from her face. Tam was so relieved and pleased that she greeted them with the warmest and most heartfelt smile.

'Thank you for seeing us. Is Matt here?' Susanne asked. 'We heard he was back.'

'I'm afraid you just missed him,' Tam explained. 'Can I help you at all?'

'We just wanted to thank him. He put us in touch with the British Association of Adoption and Fostering and we've already taken the first steps towards adopting a child.'

They held hands and looked at each other lovingly. Tam could hardly believe the change in Susanne. She looked as if a great weight had been lifted from her shoulders.

It was only now that she saw the real Susanne that she realised just how broken she was on that previous visit. It was as if a miracle had occurred.

'Matt was right,' Susanne said. 'He said that Gary only wanted me to stop the IVF treatment because he loved me and couldn't bear to see how upset I was getting.'

'I've told her so many times, I married her because I loved her, not because I wanted kids,' Gary put in. 'I think she finally believes me.'

'That's wonderful,' Tam said, her joy for Susanne and Gary making her heart take flight. 'If there's anything we can do to help — '

'Just tell Matt thanks from us,' Susanne said. 'Even if our plans to adopt fall through, he made me see that there is more to marriage and loving someone than having children.'

And I accused him of being cold, Tam thought as the happy couple left.

She was still pondering how much that must have hurt him when her door flew open and Denise rushed in.

'There's been an accident, Tam,' she said. 'Adrian's already gone home, Andrew is at the gym and I can't find Matt. It's down along the coast road and the ambulance can't get through because a lorry has jack-knifed across the main road into town. They're trying to muster the air ambulance, but the weather is pretty dicey and they're not sure it'll be able to land. The police are on their way.'

Tam was out of her chair and reaching for her bag long before Denise had finished speaking.

'What sort of accident is it?' she asked, hurrying out of her office.

'Traffic,' Denise said, then she hesitated before saying the words that brought an instant chill to Tam's heart. 'I think it might be a motorbike.'

Tam stopped dead. Her blood ran cold. Denise had pressed her lips together, her eyes wide.

'Motorbike? And you say you couldn't get hold of Matt?'

'There are a lot of bikes around here,' Denise said, unconvincingly.

If anything had happened to him, Tam would never forgive herself. She told him she didn't and never had loved him. It was the biggest lie of her life.

9

The rain was driven in by a strengthening easterly wind. Tam could barely see through her windscreen as she drove down the road and then she rounded a bend and saw the flashing blue lights of a police car.

And there was Matt's bike, lying on its side beside the road. The big powerful red machine, downed like a wounded beast. She pulled in and got out of her car as one of the police officers came towards her.

'You'll have to turn back,' he shouted above the roar of the wind. 'The road is going to be blocked for a while.'

'I'm a doctor,' she yelled back. 'Where is . . . ' Matt's name stuck in her throat. 'What's the situation?'

'A doctor?' he repeated. 'Thank God! We've only just got here ourselves. We'll sort out the traffic if you can check the casualties. The motorcyclist looks bad, but the old couple in the car just seem to be a bit shaken. We're trying to get an ambulance through, but it's going to be a while. I'm afraid we're on our own for now.'

Tam nodded, taking it all in, planning her first move. Her priority had to be the motorcycle casualty.

Matt's life could depend on her holding it together. But the sight of his bike lying there was terrifying.

Tam forced herself to take in the scene. A car had also been involved and was up on the verge. Two more cars were pulled up further down the road, hazard lights flashing.

'This way,' the officer said, leading her towards a figure slumped on the ground. 'Do you need any help?'

Tam stared at the policeman for a moment, rain washing down her face, running in a stream from her nose. Help? It looked as if she might need a miracle. She fought back rising hysteria and kept her voice calm.

'I can manage,' she said, knowing that until further help arrived his priority was to keep the scene safe. 'But I may need help in a while. I'll call.'

Her heart hammered as she looked down at the still form heaped at the side of the road beneath a blanket. At least someone had thought to keep him warm.

'Oh, Matt,' she whispered and bit hard onto her lip.

The doctor in her kicked in. She rubbed the back of her hand across her face and fell to her knees on the sodden grass beside the casualty, blinking the rain from her eyes.

Safety was not an issue. The police were dealing with that. She moved on to the next stage. Response.

'Can you hear me?' she said clearly. 'You don't have to speak, just squeeze my hand.'

She clasped a wet, bloodied hand and the fingers closed around hers and squeezed minutely. It was almost enough to make her go limp with relief.

At least he was conscious — and that was something of a miracle, given the extent of his injuries.

'Thank God,' she whispered and moved swiftly on.

'Hurts,' a muffled voice said. He lifted his hand weakly to his helmet.

'We'll leave your helmet on for the time being,' she said.

She grabbed scissors from her bag and began to cut away his clothes, exposing the wounds. The wound that concerned her most was on his thigh where his jeans were already saturated with blood. If she didn't stop the bleeding, he would bleed to death here on the wet grass. She wasn't about to let that happen.

'I'm going to have to apply a constrictive bandage,' she called out, hoping the police officer would hear her. 'I need help. Can you just give me a hand for a moment?'

She felt someone arrive at her side and hoped that the police officer had a strong stomach. 'Thank you,' she said calmly, then spoke once more to the casualty. 'Are you still with us?'

A muffled 'Yes.'

'Good. You hang in there.'

She wanted to tell him she loved him — that he was the only man she had ever or would ever love. She wanted to tell him that in case he died, because she didn't want him to die thinking that she hated him.

'Stay with me now. Stay awake. I know it's hard . . . I know it hurts, but just stay with me.'

It took every ounce of her will to keep her voice brisk and steady.

Then she checked her watch, bit the cap off her pen and wrote the exact time on a patch of skin that she'd quickly wiped free of blood.

'That's so they'll know at the hospital how long the tourniquet has been in place,' she explained to the police officer.

'I know,' he said in a painfully familiar voice. 'Good job. Are you okay?'

She felt the gentle weight of a hand on her shoulder. It wasn't the policeman at her side at all. It was Matt.

She hardly dared turn round. Was she dreaming? But when she did turn, he was there, kneeling down beside her, concern written all over his face. His forehead was creased in a frown and rain ran down his face in torrents as he blinked back the moisture from his eyes.

'Matt!' she cried. 'I thought . . . '

'He stole my bike,' he muttered, but he didn't sound angry, just despairing. 'It was my own fault. I was going to go out on it, but didn't get any further than the gate, because I knew I was in no mood to ride responsibly. Thank God I left the helmet there with the bike as well as the stupid keys.'

She was staring at him. His hair was plastered to his head, rain was gushing down his face, but he'd never looked so beautiful — or so alive.

She couldn't tear her eyes away from

him, her gaze taking in every living part of him.

'You're all right,' she whispered, her hands reaching to cup his face, her gaze intensifying. 'Thank God, you're all right.'

'Shame the same can't be said for him,' Matt said grimly. 'Damn fool, risking throwing his life away just because he wanted to ride the bike. How is he? Apart from the obvious?'

She came to her senses in a heartbeat. It was no use kneeling here in the rain rejoicing that Matt was alive when she had a patient needing her help.

They were so absorbed that neither of them noticed the arrival of the ambulance until the paramedics appeared beside them.

Matt quickly apprised them of the situation and the extent of the injuries before he and Tam stepped back to allow them to take over.

'Let's see to these other people,' Matt said as he turned away. It had only been a matter of minutes since Tam had first arrived on the scene, yet it felt like hours.

How it had all changed. There were three police cars in attendance now and the elderly couple were sitting in one of the cars belonging to the witnesses. The night was speared with flashing blue lights and the whole scene had taken on an air of unreality.

Matt stood looking down at his bike. It had come out of the accident relatively unscathed, but after what had happened, he wasn't sure he'd feel like getting back on it again.

'What made him think he could handle a machine like this?' he said.

'Who knows,' Tam said. 'Come on, I'll drive you home. You're soaked through.'

'Thanks,' he said. 'But I think I'd better drive.'

'I'm fine,' she said.

'No, you're not,' he contradicted her. 'You're still shaking. Come on, give me your keys.'

Tam was soaked through to her skin

and her clothes were caked in mud and worse, but she didn't seem to notice. She fumbled in her pocket, pulled out the keys and immediately dropped them on the ground.

'Sorry.'

Her teeth were chattering. She was in shock. Matt remembered how he'd felt when he'd pulled her out of the water only to have her sucked from his grasp. That awful moment when he thought she'd gone forever. She had thought the body under the blanket was him — had she felt that same agonising terror?

The sooner he got her home and into the warm, the better.

'All right?' he asked as she pulled up outside Bay House.

'I'm fine, I'm fine,' she said dismissively. 'But what about you? Are you quite sure you're going to be all right?' She sounded genuinely concerned.

'Why shouldn't I be?' he said. 'It's you I'm worried about. You've had quite a shock.'

'Me?' she said, her voice rising

slightly. 'I'm fine. I just thought it was you lying beside the road in a heap. I thought . . . ' she looked down. 'I thought you were as good as dead, Matt.'

She began to shake even more violently.

'I know, love,' he said. 'I know.'

He made a move to embrace her, thought better of it and hesitated, but she was falling apart here. What was he supposed to do? Ignore her? He couldn't do that.

And when he did put his arms around her, she sobbed against his chest.

'It's always worse when it's someone you know,' he said.

'I know.' Her voice was muffled.

'You're in a worse state than me,' he said, kissing the top of her head. 'I'll take you in and hand you over to Moira. She'll take care of you.'

⋆ ⋆ ⋆

When the alarm went off the next morning, Tam had to untangle herself from the sheets. She'd hardly slept at all for tossing and turning, and every time she closed her eyes, she saw that heap at the side of the road. Only it wasn't a stranger, it was Matt — and she had his blood on her hands.

She rubbed her eyes. Her first thought was for the injured boy. Had he made it through the night?

She got out of bed and looked out of the window. The sea was as still and flat as glass and the sky was blue and cloudless. It was more like a warm June day than one in April.

'You look lovely this morning, dear,' Aunt Moira said warmly when she arrived at the breakfast table. 'If a little tired,' she added, more worriedly.

Uncle Andrew had already eaten his healthy bowl of porridge and was reading the newspaper.

'No Jack and Sally?' she asked.

Moira smiled. 'No sign of them,' she answered. 'I expect Jack is feeling a bit jet-lagged.'

Tam smiled too. Jet-lagged? Sledge-hammered, more like. Yesterday evening he'd seemed to be in a state of shock himself, as if the strength of his love for Sally and their unborn child had come as a complete surprise to him. He was still the cousin she loved, but he was different. Nicer.

'You're just in time,' Moira said as she placed a plate of scrambled eggs and bacon in front of Tam.

'I'm really not very hungry,' Tam said. The sight of the food, although good, made her throat tighten.

'Nonsense,' Moira said. 'You have to eat. You didn't eat anything last night. No wonder you're so thin.'

'I'll eat it,' Uncle Andrew said at once, folding his paper and placing it to one side.

'You will not,' Moira said sharply. 'You had maple syrup in your porridge, I saw you.'

'So? There's nothing unhealthy about what you've cooked there,' he said despairingly. 'Grilled bacon, scrambled eggs . . . '

'You see, Tam, you have to eat it,' Moira said. 'Otherwise he will, and it's not good for him.'

Tam was about to protest again when Matt walked in through the back door. She stared at him. He had never looked so wonderful.

'That looks delicious,' he said.

'Eat it,' Tam said, sliding the plate across the table.

He raised an eyebrow.

'Please,' Tam said. 'You'll be doing me a favour and saving Uncle Andrew from himself.'

'In that case,' Matt said, seating himself at the table. 'If it is for the good of all, then I have no choice.'

Moira smiled. She was happy as long as the food got eaten by anyone other than her husband.

He smiled at Tam. 'I thought you would like to know,' he said. 'I've just come from the hospital. Apart from shattered legs, a broken arm and some cracked ribs our boy is doing fine.'

'Doesn't sound very fine to me,' Moira said.

'He was lucky,' Matt said. 'No head, neck or spinal injuries. And our elderly couple were allowed to go home with their daughter last night, upset of course, but happily unscathed.'

'Thank goodness,' Tam sighed.

'No, thank *you*,' he said. 'It was your prompt actions that saved him from bleeding to death.'

'But you . . . '

'But nothing,' Matt said. 'By the time I got there, you'd already got it under control.'

He turned to Moira. 'Jack and Sally getting on all right?' he asked.

'Better than all right,' Moira said. 'They're setting a wedding date.'

'Already?' Matt's eyebrows rose. 'Better than I hoped. You must be over the moon.'

'We are,' Moira said. 'Happy endings all round.'

Moira looked meaningfully and hopefully at Tam, then at Matt. Her message was clear, but a happy ending for them was out of the question.

'I should go,' Tam said, getting up from the table. 'Please excuse me.'

* * *

After surgery that evening, Tam took a walk down the road to where the accident had happened. She stood staring at the scars in the road, the gouged grass and the bits and pieces of shattered vehicle that had been moved to one side.

It could have been Matt.

'Thought I'd find you here,' Matt said. He put his arm around her. 'You all right? Tell me what you're thinking, Tam.'

It was now or never.

'I hoped to keep it from you, but I can't any longer. I do love you — so much, but we can't have a future together and I owe it to you to explain.'

Her words made his heart smash against his ribs. What was she going to say? What could possibly have happened to prevent them having a future together?

'I'll take you to Bay Cottage,' he said, his voice little more than a croak. 'I'll call Moira and tell her you're having dinner with me tonight and we'll talk. Okay?'

'Yes,' she murmured. 'That would be best.'

'And perhaps you'll let me decide whether or not we have a future — or at least have a say in that decision?'

'I think when you've heard what I have to say, that you'll agree with me,' she said dully.

⋆ ⋆ ⋆

Tam stood in Matt's cosy living room and watched him as he made the call to Aunt Moira.

'All sorted,' he said, putting the phone down and coming towards her. 'Oh, Tam . . . you look so lost.'

'Let me show you something, Matt,' she said. She couldn't find the words to say it, so she pulled down the front of her trousers.

Matt stared at the scar on her stomach. 'You didn't have that a year ago,' he said, swallowing the lump in his throat. 'What happened?'

He traced it with his finger. This was no minor surgery; this was serious stuff. His eyes rose to meet hers and he saw she was crying.

'Oh, love, don't cry,' he said, enfolding her in his arms.

'It wasn't meant to be like this,' Tam sobbed. 'I didn't want you to know about it. Ever.'

'Know what, love? What happened to you?'

He sat down on the sofa with her and held her close. 'Tell me.'

'I was pregnant,' she said so quietly he could barely hear. He closed his eyes. The pain was indescribable. He didn't want to hear this, but he knew he had to.

'I didn't realise . . . the pain, the bleeding . . . it was Cara who saved me. She knew almost at once what was wrong.'

'Oh no,' he said as the truth finally began to dawn. The realisation of just how tragically wrong he'd been about her hit him with the force of a sledgehammer.

'I'd been nauseous too, but I thought it was jet-lag,' she said wryly, mocking herself. 'Some doctor, eh, Matt?'

'Ectopic,' he murmured. It wasn't a question. He knew it had been a sentence of death for their baby. A death she'd had to face all alone. His heart ached for her, the grief and pain she must have endured.

He kissed her face softly, waiting for her to continue.

'It was bad, Matt,' she went on. 'They tried to repair the tube, but the damage was too great. And then I got a post-operative infection. My other tube was damaged. I was . . . um . . . pretty ill.'

'Pretty ill?' he murmured, shocked. 'Tam, I could have lost you forever. Why didn't you tell me? I would have come to you. Does Moira know?'

'She's the only one,' Tam said. 'I swore her to secrecy.'

'But why?' he pleaded, cupping her face in his hands and turning her to face him. 'Why didn't you tell me?'

Her eyes brimmed with tears. 'Because I love you so much, Matt,' she said. 'I couldn't bear not to be able to give you the family you long for.'

'Do you honestly think I want a family that much that I'd be willing to sacrifice a whole future with you? Tam, I would rather have you and nothing else in this world, than live the rest of my life without you. And if you still want children, there are alternatives.'

She made to protest, but he pressed his finger against her lips.

'I know many couples who are perfectly happy without children because they have each other and nothing else matters.'

'Oh, Matt . . . '

'Marry me, Tam. I want you, only you. Children would be a wonderful gift, but we don't need them to be happy. All we need is each other.'

He bent his head and kissed her soft yielding lips, tasting the bittersweet salt of her tears. He had never loved this much, this completely, in all his life.

10

It was as perfect a summer day as Moira could hope for on the day of the Sea Festival that August. Tam had woken early to the sounds of early-bird children laughing and squealing as they played on the sand at the base of the cliffs. A lone gull cried long and loud as if to say, 'Come on sleepyheads, get out of bed!' And from Bay House next door, she could hear the distant wail of a hungry baby crying for his morning feed.

Beside her, Matt stirred and wrapped a strong, bare arm around her waist. 'Mmm,' he murmured with a sleepy smile as he cuddled up close and nuzzled her neck. 'Let's not get up today.'

She lifted his arm, kissed his hand and jumped out of bed before he could persuade her to stay. *Not that I'd need much persuading*, she thought as she looked down at him.

'Come on,' she laughed. 'We've got so much to do today. There's no time for lazing in bed.'

He sat up and grinned and she could have sworn her heart stopped in its tracks. 'We've got ages yet,' he said with a sexy smile that made her stomach churn with longing.

'Oh, you.' Tam picked up her pillow and hit him with it and he grabbed her round the waist and pulled her back down on the bed.

As their laughter mingled, Tam thought she might burst with happiness.

A few hours later, the sun was still beating down from a cloudless Wedgwood-blue sky and the water in the harbour twinkled.

Tam stood by the harbour wall with her aunt and uncle, and Sally and Jack's gorgeous baby.

'There's Jack with our ice creams,' Andrew said.

'Let's go then,' Moira said cheerfully as she turned the pushchair and adjusted the sunshade so that her sleeping grandson was in shadow. 'Do you want to have a push, Grandpa?'

'Don't mind if I do,' Andrew chuckled as he reached for the handles. 'As long as you don't think I'll be overdoing things. You will excuse us, won't you, Tam?'

They'd fallen right into the role of grandparents and were enjoying every minute. And wanting to spend time with his grandchild had given Andrew the excuse he needed to retire.

Tam was smiling to herself as she watched them walk away. They were looking better, both of them — far less frail and worn than a few months ago.

The starting pistol was fired and the raft race began. There were twenty rafts taking part, including one cobbled together by Adrian and Matt which sank about twenty metres from the start line, to roars of laughter and cheers from the onlookers lined along the harbour wall.

She handed Matt a towel when he joined her. She still couldn't quite believe that they were married. It had been a quiet wedding, and she knew he was going to be a wonderful husband and an even better father. Not that he knew it yet — but he soon would.

'I have something to tell you later,' she said teasingly and Matt gave her a quizzical look, his head cocked slightly to one side.

She'd done not one but two tests when she got up this morning. Against all the odds, they were going to be parents. She'd been told the chances of her getting pregnant were remote — not impossible, but highly unlikely.

'What's that?' he asked.

'You'll find out,' Tam teased. 'We'd better watch the rest of the race.'

Matt pulled her close. She stared up at him and for a moment she couldn't believe how lucky she was to be so in love, and to have that love returned.

And there was the new life blossoming inside her.

'I love you so much,' she whispered.

'I love you too,' he replied fiercely.

And then he kissed her while tumultuous applause and cheers for the racers rang out around them. They would have their happy ending after all.

We do hope that you have enjoyed reading this large print book.

Did you know that all of our titles are available for purchase?

We publish a wide range of high quality large print books including:
Romances, Mysteries, Classics
General Fiction
Non Fiction and Westerns

Special interest titles available in large print are:
The Little Oxford Dictionary
Music Book, Song Book
Hymn Book, Service Book

Also available from us courtesy of Oxford University Press:
Young Readers' Dictionary
(large print edition)
Young Readers' Thesaurus
(large print edition)

For further information or a free brochure, please contact us at:

Other titles in the
Linford Romance Library:

CHERRY BLOSSOM

Patricia Keyson

Cherry's narrow boat home is sinking and she's persuaded to stay in a chalet at the hotel where she works. Cherry is smitten with the rather distant owner, Oliver. And despite his cool and aloof manner, she has never felt such passion, even towards her ex-husband. Oliver's brother, Darius, is far easier company. Whatever happens, she will always put the welfare of her son, Jay, first. Who will Cherry choose?

HOLD ON TO YOUR DREAMS

Karen Abbott

Following her father's financial ruin and the untimely deaths of both her parents, Emily's comfortable life in Society comes to an end. Her pride prevents her from letting the man she loves know that her feelings for him are unchanged, so she throws herself upon the mercies of her aunt — a malicious woman. Although forced to work as a servant, Emily's dreams linger on. Will she ever regain her position in Society and her lost love?

SWINGS AND ROUNDABOUTS

Wendy Kremer

Damián Alvarez is a man targeted by the paparazzi. A top professional Spanish golfer, he's dynamic, wealthy and impulsive. When he meets Emma McKay he employs her to organise his travel arrangements and control the press. She accompanies him and his entourage on the world circuit, and, despite her resolve, falls for Damián — but then his one-time girlfriend shows up. Is Damián capable of real devotion to one woman? If so, which one will it be?

THE RED EARTH

June Gadsby

Lexi takes a huge risk going to Kenya to marry a man she hardly knows. It seems only to be expected that her fiancé's family will, initially, be suspicious about her. After all, they are part of the wealthy elite, whereas she is an unknown quantity. However, she's not prepared for the attitude of her arrogant, controlling future brother-in-law. Morgan Tyler seems prepared to stop at nothing to make her feel unwelcome. But Fate plays tricks on them both . . .

FOR THE CHILDREN'S SAKE

Teresa Ashby

Cathy Galliani wakes in hospital, after a car accident, to learn that her husband Vittorio is dead and her stepchildren are with his family in Italy. She is visited in hospital by Dan Kirby, a witness to the accident. Cathy travels to Italy to see the children, but when Dan follows her he ends up in hospital himself. And as his life hangs in the balance, Cathy realises how deeply he cares for her — and who he really is . . .

NO MISTAKING LOVE

Moyra Tarling

Working at Moonbeam Lake, it wasn't easy for single mother Laura Matthews. She wanted her twins to enjoy summer in the place she'd once loved — despite its painful memories. But she hadn't counted on Tanner Mcleod's reappearance. Six years ago, she'd comforted him when his brother died, and it had led to passion. But Tanner had left before she'd discovered the consequences of their love. How could she confess that HE was the father the twins had never met?